UNWITTING

BY
STEVEN CANTER

This a work of fiction. Names, characters, places, and inci-
dents either are the product of the author's imagination or
are used fictitiously. Any resemblance to actual persons,
liv-ing or dead, events, or locales is entirely coincidental.

DEDICATION

To the Instructors at The School

Your training kept me alive.

To my Family

Your love kept me sane.

CHAPTER 1

Making order out of chaos.
Sometimes it requires a high body count.

He sat very still on the bench by the Potomac. He was practiced in being still.

A light breeze teased the surface of the river into faint ripples. The rusty hand-railing between himself and the water offended his view, like a knife slash across a Renoir.

He had the appearance of a mid-level executive on a lunch break, but he wasn't. His graying hair, buzzed short, and his tanned, weathered face created the backdrop for his intense, alert eyes. Someone had once called his eyes *experienced,* as if all he had seen was reflected there. He knew that statement wasn't true because people didn't flee in fear after making eye contact.

Dave Walsh had been well-trained by the US government.

He had spent thirty of his fifty-five years at nearly full throttle, traveling to every unglamorous, hot, smelly, shithole on the planet, where people tried their best to kill him.

Dave Walsh had been the best, at one time.

Six months ago, retirement had seemed like a good idea, a graceful way to step off the operational merry-go-round that never stopped spinning.

Now, he was weary.

Dave had more than enough money to survive and no immediate family to share his newfound time off with. He'd convinced himself that he would fill that time pursuing his hobbies; however, the reality was that his current "hobbies" were all solo pursuits, wedged in between sporadic deployment schedules that, in his mind, prevented him from committing to "team" activities. Maybe he just preferred doing things on his own.

For the first time in his adult life, Dave had been in control of his own schedule, and for six months, he'd forcibly filled that time with various activities. He'd sought solace by riding his motorcycle across the country, stopping in the Smoky Mountains to fly fish and camp. He'd spent a week at the range burning a thousand rounds through his Glock 19 to maintain his 1.3-second draw and head shot. He'd even begun taking flying lessons.

But it all seemed hollow. He soon realized that he needed a sense of mission and a sense of urgency to feel relevant.

To Dave, life without relevance was a meaningless existence.

His former employer wanted him to return as an independent contractor. But Dave wasn't sure he was ready to jump back into the operational world as an *extra,* and not the main character. Dave's consistent record of success was so strong that once given an assignment, he was allowed to make unilateral decisions to complete the mission. He was known as a "fire and forget missile." He knew that his solo operational style had been the key to his success, and to his survival.

Dave found himself spending more and more time trying to clarify his next move. He could identify with the rusty railing he was staring at: *worn, but still useful.*

* * *

Movement to his right and slightly behind him, just at the edge of his peripheral vision, brought him back to the present.

A half-turn of his head and an eye tap for threat assessment.

The movement came from a disheveled young girl—early twenties, street skinny, dirty blonde hair, white dress ending just below her knees, black Vans, no socks. She was walking directly toward his bench. He looked at her hands. *"The hands, or what they hold, can kill you."* After all the years as an operator, the voices of his training instructors still echoed in his head.

She had a man's briefcase clutched to her chest. That odd juxtaposition dictated a harder look. Dave turned and looked beyond her, running a visual pattern ranging from near to far. Shrubs, trees, vehicles, and windows: he saw no one trying to hide, no "too casual" looking park-walkers, no rifles intersecting the roof lines.

Perhaps the girl was a street person who had stolen a briefcase?

His internal threat level reduced a notch.

The girl sat down on the end of the bench, breathing hard and staring straight ahead. She clutched the

3

briefcase like a flight attendant demonstrating the use of a seat cushion for flotation. She was trying, but failing, to blend in. Tears stained her cheeks.

For a split second, his deep brain subconscious floated an idea by his conscious brain.

Sarah?

But it couldn't be Sarah. Sarah was dead.

Don't get involved, he told himself.

Her frailness and fear and the similarity to his daughter, Sarah, triggered his protective nature. Intellectually, he knew better than to insert himself in someone else's problems. But that would be like expecting a sheepdog to not protect the flock.

"Are you okay?" he asked. The girl flinched and spun her head toward him. She hadn't noticed that someone was sitting on the other end of the bench. Her mouth opened and closed several times; her eyes were wide and unfocused. She was in shock. As she lowered the briefcase slightly, Dave noticed blood stains on the front of her dress.

His threat level spiked; he felt his scalp prickle and his pulse quicken.

New assessment of the girl … *Is she a decoy? A distraction meant to hold my attention while I'm attacked?*

Once again, he rapidly scanned for threats, but observed nothing out of sync.

"Are you hurt?" he asked, his eyes still scanning the area.

She shook her head slowly.

"Will you tell me what happened?" he asked, afraid she would spook and bolt like a frightened deer.

She looked at the briefcase and then back up at him. "He, uh, handed it to me . . . and told me to run," she stammered. "He was holding his stomach and there was blood, lots of blood, on his shirt and his hands."

The blood on her clothes was a transfer, not hers.

He knew with certainty that someone would be coming for her any minute.

They needed to move.

"Can you walk?" he asked.

She nodded.

To help manage the effects of shock and to change her appearance, even if only slightly, he removed his jacket and put it over her shoulders. Dave put his hands on the briefcase and she surrendered it to him like it was an evil talisman.

Movement across the street caught his attention: one guy, khaki pants, navy blue jacket, light blue shirt, head swiveling right and left. He had not looked their way—yet.

Dave gently helped the girl to her feet and guided her away from the bench. In spite of the urgency to leave the area, they walked. *Running attracted attention.* Moving laterally to stay out of the man's line of sight, Dave worked to keep trees or shrubs between themselves and the man. The man raised a handheld radio to his lips and spoke into it. Within seconds, a black SUV screeched to a halt in front of him. Dave could see him shake his head as he talked to the driver through the lowered window.

The girl also saw the man and the SUV and she suddenly stopped walking, frozen in fear. Dave attempted to guide her away by placing his hand on her upper arm, but to no avail. He knew they couldn't stand there long.

5

He leaned in. Using the soft voice he'd used with his daughter, he said, "My name is Dave. What's yours?" She turned to him and wrinkled her brow as if he had just addressed her in some foreign language. "What's your name?" he asked again.

"Lydia," she said, barely audible.

"Lydia, I can help you. You'll be safe. Walk with me."

Searching his eyes, he could tell that she sensed something she seldom experienced on the street: sincerity and confidence. Against her nature, Lydia seemed to trust him. She nodded as they began moving again.

Dave began a surveillance detection route to lose the pursuers. Entering one of the stores that lined the park, Dave nodded to the sales clerk as if he owned the place. They quickly walked to the rear of the shop and out the back door before the clerk could voice the surprise registering on her face.

Dave turned left. *Studies had shown that most people fleeing turned right when presented with an option.* He worked his way through the alleys, always angling away from the last known sighting of his pursuers, putting distance and structures between them and him. He glanced skyward and listened—no airplanes or helicopters: all good, so far.

After putting several blocks between himself and the pursuers, he pulled the girl into a small café filled with tourists. It would offer temporary anonymity.

He ordered a coffee for him and a coke for her: she needed sugar to counter the shock. Sitting with his back to the rear wall, he maintained a clear view of the front entrance. He placed the briefcase on the floor under the table and casually scanned the sidewalk in front of the café through the large, plate glass windows.

Dave stood up and said, "Sit here for one minute. Don't move. I'll be right back." Lydia flinched as a flash of panic crossed her face.

"I'm just going to check for a back door," he reassured her. He walked quickly down the hall, locating it twenty steps from his table.

The server was setting their drinks in front of them just as he returned. Lydia picked up hers with a shaky hand and took a sip. She closed her eyes for a minute. Hating to break her solitude, but needing more information, Dave urged, "Now, tell me what happened."

This time, she found her voice.

"I'd been to the used bookstore on Pennsylvania and was walking home. I saw this man staggering on the sidewalk. At first, I thought he was drunk, but his face was really sweaty and he looked like he was in pain.

"So, I thought maybe he was having a heart attack or something. He was holding a briefcase against his chest. He saw me and said something. I asked, 'What?' and he said, 'Take this,' and he pushed his briefcase towards me. I didn't understand. He said, 'Take this and run.' Now I was, like, freaking out, and thought maybe this was some kind of TV joke and they were filming me.

"Then I saw these two men turn the corner and start running toward him. He shoved the briefcase into my arms. I tried to back away, but the look in his eyes . . . he was desperate. He was begging me. He took a step back, and I saw he was covered with blood. He looked like he'd been stabbed or something.

"I didn't know what to do. He said, 'Run!' The men were getting closer. I was scared, so I just turned and ran toward the park until I didn't see them anymore. I sat on the bench to catch my breath and you were there."

CHAPTER 2

Dave reached under the café table and retrieved the briefcase.

What could be important enough to stab someone, in broad daylight, in the middle of the sidewalk? A drug deal gone bad? Was the stabbing just a random act of violence? No, that wouldn't explain the search team. The public assault and the immediate search had a feeling of organization behind it.

Dave put the case on the table between himself and Lydia and examined it. It was an expensive, hard-sided leather briefcase, and it looked fairly new—no scuff marks. The case was locked and had a three-digit number beneath each hasp. He tried a few random combinations, but none of them worked. He pulled a special knife from his pocket that held six lock-picks folded into a three-inch-long handle. It was illegal to carry, but he was really good with locks and it beat keeping spare keys scattered around. Dave selected one of the picks and had the brief-case open in less than a minute.

Slowly opening the case, he took a look at the single item in the center, closed his eyes, and quietly uttered one word: "Shit!" He closed the case and placed his hand on top of it.

Lydia, watching his face, had been unable to see the contents. She asked, "What? What is it?"

Dave turned the case and opened it just enough for her to see an object strapped inside, held with Velcro. It was a small brass cylinder comprised of five narrow, numbered wheels. It looked like some kind of number puzzle. She didn't understand.

Turning the case back, he reached in and pulled the object free. "This is a Cryptex safe that contains a USB flash drive. These wheels spin to line up the numbers for a combination. Inside is a memory stick."

"What's it for?"

"The government keeps top secret information on drives like this. Normally, they never let them out of their possession."

Using his pocket knife, he cut the corner of the suede material lining the briefcase. Pulling the material away revealed a cutout in the bottom of the case that contained a tiny electronic box with a small red LED light—probably a tracking device. He pocketed the Cryptex safe, closed and relocked the briefcase, and placed it back under the table.

"We really need to leave—now!" He placed a ten-dollar bill on the table as he stood up.

"Can't I stay here?" she asked. "You take the case—I don't want it. I didn't even know that guy and I don't have anything to do with this. I just want to stay here. You take it and go."

As if in answer to her question, the big SUV they had seen earlier screeched to a halt in front of the building. Six men, dressed from head to toe in black, leaped out. They had pistols drawn and were headed toward the front door.

Dave calmly looked at Lydia, waiting for her decision. She looked from him to the front door and back. "Don't leave me!" she said.

He searched her eyes for a moment and with two words, he fully committed. "Let's go." She followed him down the hall and out the back.

Dave and Lydia had just rounded the back corner of the building, heading to Dave's truck, when two of the men from the SUV stormed through the front door of the café.

Customers screamed.

The men began yelling, "Hands on the table! No phones. No phones!" Their eyes swept the café, guns drawn. Quickly spotting the locked briefcase under the table, one of them immediately grabbed it.

The one who seemed to be in charge—a big, weight-lifter type with a flattop haircut—asked a customer at the next table, "Who was sitting here?"

A twenty-something guy sitting with his girlfriend tried to play cool and answered, "I'm not sure."

"Did you see who was sitting here?" Flattop asked. No answer. Flattop stared at the young man for a count of five, looked away for one second, and then without warning, spun back and punched him in the face. The blow knocked the kid and his chair over backward, his head smacking the floor like a dropped stack of books.

The four remaining men on the sidewalk had split into two teams. One team took up position outside the front door, preventing the curious from entering the café; the other team began moving down the block toward the back of the building. One man guarded the door from the inside, preventing anyone from leaving.

Flattop reached down, grabbed a handful of the boy's t-shirt, and pulled him to his feet.

"I'm going to ask you one more time . . . describe the person sitting at that table."

"A guy and a girl," the frightened boy said. He moved his hand to the back of his head and pulled it away to reveal that it was wet with blood. Tears flooded his eyes.

"Are you saying a *guy* was with the girl? What did they look like?" Flattop asked.

"Yes, a guy was with her. The guy was older than the girl. She looked skinny and had dirty hair," he said, through sniffles.

"What were they wearing?" Flattop asked in a serious monotone.

"I'm not s-sure. Maybe he was wearing a light blue shirt, and she had on a dark jacket. I wasn't paying that much attention," the kid whined.

"Did you see them leave?" Flattop asked.

"No. No, I didn't. They were sitting there, then you guys came in, and now they're gone."

Flattop pointed to the man guarding the front door and inclined his head toward the back hall. The man took off at a jog. Within seconds, Flattop's radio crackled, "*No joy.*" He brought the radio to his mouth and spoke one word, "Exfil."

The men exited the café and climbed into the SUV, the doors slamming shut as it jerked away from the curb.

Marcus, the flat-topped team leader, held the briefcase in his lap. He was under strict orders not to open it.

The tracking device in the case had led them to the café. Picking up his secure, handheld radio, he keyed the mic and called the Tactical Operations Center (TOC).

"Archangel, this is Gabriel, over."

"Go for Archangel," the radio squawked.

"Article recovered. In-bound at this time," Marcus replied.

"Roger, Gabriel. We will meet you in the team room. Out."

CHAPTER 3

Dave knew it was time to call Jax.

Jax was Jackson Baer. They had served together in a lot of sketchy places. They'd done some nasty things to some nasty people. At times, it felt like the most remarkable thing they'd done was survive.

Ten Years Earlier

Dave was driving; Jax was riding shotgun in their dirty white Toyota Hilux.

They were barely moving through the streets of the "Mog" or Mogadishu, Somalia, on their way to meet with a high-ranking member of the Hawiye clan. The Hawiyes were the largest and the most dominant clan in Mogadishu. The clan member they were to meet supposedly had information on the newly-forming radical youth wing, Al-Shabaab.

It was hot. It was always hot in Mogadishu, and it always smelled like shit and burning charcoal in the land that even God had apparently abandoned. The windows were rolled up to keep someone from lobbing a grenade into the truck. The truck's meager air conditioner was putting forth a valiant effort to supply cool air and it was failing impressively.

Both men were sweat-soaked and heavily armed.

A Glock 19 rode a Kydex holster concealed under a large, untucked shirt. Collapsible-stock M4 rifles were positioned barrel down beside their legs, keeping the weapons out of view of passersby. Since wearing the bulky vests while riding around town would make the men stand out, their armored web vests were stored under a tarp on the back floorboard of the truck. Brown makeup, rubbed on their already deeply tanned hands and faces, darkened their skin. Oakley sunglasses and sweat-stained baseball caps completed the look.

If you stood out, you were a target. If you were a target, you usually died.

They inched down a narrow street with vendors lining both sides. Lots of slow-moving traffic. Lots of people walking. Lots of vehicles. Lots of guns. Lots of noise: car horns blowing, loud voices, tinny speakers at full volume playing songs heavy with the oud.

Dave and Jax tuned out most of the environmental background noise and scanned constantly for threats with each man owning a "clock" sector relevant to their position in the vehicle. They'd been creeping along at a walking pace for about thirty minutes. The crowd had almost completely dispersed for about a block in front of them—not a single person on the streets. That was different from normal.

"Different" typically meant danger.

"Twelve o'clock," Dave said.

Jax understood immediately. "Slow," was all he said.

Dave pushed in the clutch and started tapping the brake pedal, slowing the small truck even more.

Jax saw him first. "Foot-mobile with a cell phone on the roof to the right."

Maybe the triggerman for an ambush.

"Got him," Dave replied.

Jax saw an abandoned vendor's cart parked on the edge of the street; that wasn't normal either. Realization hit.

"Stop! Stop! Stop!" he yelled.

Dave stomped the brakes just as the cart vaporized in a huge, dirty brown explosion. They had avoided the ambush kill-zone by mere yards. The explosion rocked the Hilux, but didn't overturn it.

Debris from the metal vendor cart slammed into the front of the truck, cracking the windshield and shredding the front tires. The men were enveloped in a choking cloud of dust as pieces of glass from the shattered side windows cut their faces, their ballistic sunglasses saving their eyes. The pungent smell of HME created unwanted olfactory memories.

"*Go! Go! Go!*" Jax yelled, as he used his hand to push down on Dave's right leg that was on the gas pedal. They had to move immediately out of the kill-zone. *Get off the X! Get off the X!* The blast had wrecked the tires and the engine; the truck wouldn't move.

"Vehicle down!" yelled Dave. Both men had been temporarily deafened by the blast. Then they heard: *tink, tink, tink, tink* as rounds began hitting the left side of the truck. The rear side window shattered.

"Contact left, contact left!" they yelled simultaneously.

Jax quickly scanned out the right side of the truck before opening the door to make sure he was not stepping into gunfire. Seeing no immediate threat, he pulled the handle, pushed the door open with his boot, and grabbed his rifle on the way out. Having practiced this emergency action drill a thousand times, their response was immediate. No thinking, just reaction.

Jax exited the door, unfolded his six-foot-two frame, and moved quickly toward the front of the truck, bringing his rifle to his shoulder while scanning for targets. He took up a position just behind the front fender, using the engine block and front wheel for cover.

Jax quickly identified two shooters in the building across the street, on the left side of the road, one at ground level and one on the roof. He moved back about three feet from the truck, dropped to one knee as he raised his rifle, sighted over the top of his scope, and snapped off four quick rounds, two at each shooter, attempting to get them to stop shooting and move behind cover. It worked. Both ambushers retreated just long enough for him to call to Dave.

"Two skinnies. One high, one low. Engaging . . ." Jax was now peering through his rifle scope and firing at a slow but steady rate, attempting to pin the shooters down until his partner could bring his weapon on line.

By now, Dave had crawled across the passenger's seat and exited the vehicle with his rifle. He moved to the rear door, pulled it open, and retrieved both of their tactical vests. Kneeling to stay out of the line of fire, he dropped his vest over his head, fastened the Velcro straps across the front, and then transitioned his Glock from his belt holster to the holster on the front of his vest. He set the other vest beside Jax's foot and took up a shooting position at the rear fender.

"Where?" he asked Jax.

"Watch my rounds," Jax replied. He fired two rounds low and two rounds high at the positions the shooters were last seen. Dave saw the gray puffs where the rounds impacted the concrete walls.

"Got it," Dave said. He flipped open the cover of his ACOG scope with his left thumb and placed the red illuminated dot over the pockmarks Jax had created with his marking shots. He thumbed the safety off, rested the pad of his index finger on the trigger, and waited for the inevitable.

Jax bent down, grabbed his vest, pulled it over his head, and secured it.

As if scripted, the lull in the firing created a curiosity too strong for the ambushers to resist. Revealing only his head and chest, the shooter on the roof looked around the edge of a small cupola to see if the occupants of the truck were still there. With the target acquired, Dave slowly squeezed the trigger and sent a 62 grain, coppercoated bullet, traveling at three thousand feet per second through the ambusher's head. The hypervelocity round created a puff of red blood mist and the dead man dropped like all his bones had been disconnected. His AK-47 clattered off the roof and tumbled to the street below.

Dave seamlessly transitioned his aiming point to the ground floor where Jax had marked the second shooter.

"Tango on the roof is down," Dave said calmly.

"Rog," Jax acknowledged as he scanned the other sectors for threats.

Dave saw the second shooter's rifle barrel sticking around the door frame as he raised it to fire. The "tell" gave Dave a perfect lead on where the shooter's head would appear in the next half-second. He placed the red dot of his scope on the wall an inch from where his target would show. As predicted, the shemagh-covered head of the shooter peered out of the doorway, trying to line up a shot on the men behind the destroyed truck.

Dave smoothly moved his rifle two inches to the right, placing the ACOG's red dot on the center of the cloth-covered head, and shot him—a replay of the scene before. Red mist; falling man.

"Second guy's down," Dave said.

"Let's get the hell out of here," Jax replied. He made eye contact with Dave and pointed to an alley behind them. Dave nodded.

Jax turned, pointed his rifle toward the alley and said, "Moving!"

Dave answered, "Covering," while looking through his rifle scope, scanning for additional threats.

Jax stepped into the darkened alley and took cover in a kneeling position. The alley smelled like piss and rotting garbage. "Covering!" Jax relayed, once in position.

Dave pulled a backpack and a road flare from the back floor of the pickup. Slinging the backpack over his shoulder, he ignited the road flare and rolled it under the Hilux. The damaged truck was leaking fuel and it burst into flames immediately. Black, oily smoke masked their movements.

"Moving!" he called to Jax as he pivoted and ran toward the alley.

Dave took Jax's place at the mouth of the alley and dropped to one knee about a foot from the wall and two feet into the shadows.

"Calling for extract," Jax said, as he moved deeper into the alley and inserted the ear piece from the radio on his vest. As he made the call, Jax faced the rear to provide security. There had been no need to formulate this initial plan; they had been in situations like this so many times that both knew what the other was thinking.

First steps: move away from the last point of contact, continually re-assess the threat situation, make radio contact with the TOC, move to a safe location. They were working through the list.

Dave had his rifle pointed down at a forty-five-degree angle, his finger alongside the trigger guard. While scanning for threats, he conducted a tactical inventory of his gear, mentally noting his remaining ammunition.

Jax moved back up to Dave's position and said, "They'll have a vehicle-extract for us at these coordinates," pointing to his map. "It's about six blocks from here."

At that moment, a hailstorm of gunfire erupted from in front. Rounds impacted the block wall above their heads, showering them with dust and chunks of concrete. The dirt around them danced like it was raining death drops. Dave raised his rifle to counter the threat. Through the smoke of the burning truck, he could see men with guns running toward the alley, firing from the hip. They ran up, pulled the trigger to let off five or six rounds, and ran back to cover.

Dave could imagine the gunmen lost in their Khat-induced afternoon high, the chewed leaves of the green plant giving them both a false sense of courage and a buzz. Dave got off two rounds before feeling like he had been hit in his upper right arm with a baseball bat. He glanced down and saw that his shirt was ripped on the outside of his right sleeve.

"Shit, I've been shot," he said. At the same time, he heard Jax grunt behind him. He yelled over his shoulder, "Jax, you okay?"

Jax said, "Yeah, a round hit my chest plate."

As Dave continued firing at the movement across the road, he noticed Jax had yet to fire.

"Hey partner, how about putting some rounds out?" he yelled. He fired four more times, then turned to see what could possibly have Jax more occupied than this firefight.

Jax was still kneeling, but staring with unfocused eyes. Dave saw pink foam and bubbles on his lips. The round that clipped Dave's arm must have hit the edge of Jax's armor plate, broken apart, and entered his chest and lung. A lung-shot would account for the pink foamy bubbles coming from Jax's mouth. Dave knew he had to get Jax back in the fight or they would both die here.

"Hey! If it's not too much trouble, fucking shoot somebody!" he yelled.

Jax shook his head, and he seemed to come back from wherever he had been. He raised his rifle and started firing.

"Let's pull back," Jax yelled into Dave's ear, over the din of the gunfire. Dave nodded.

Jax appeared to be back in the fight. He tapped Dave on his right shoulder as he moved back to the rear of the alley. Dave continued to pour aimed fire at anything moving across the street.

Once Jax had established himself in the new position, he began firing past Dave, down the alley and into the street. Dave unhooked a smoke grenade from his web harness, pulled the pin, yelled, "Smoke out!" and lobbed the grenade into the mouth of the alley to cover his movement. As the canister spewed and spit volumes of dense white smoke, Dave pivoted to his left, toward the wall, keeping close to it as he ran in a crouch back toward Jax. He knew Jax would be firing past him down the right side of the alley and didn't want to run into his line of fire.

Dave's right arm was beginning to burn and go numb. Blood soaked his sleeve and dripped off his fingertips where he held the pistol grip of his rifle. While Jax took cover behind a stack of firewood, Dave tapped him on the shoulder as he ran past him deeper into the alley, towards an abandoned car body mounted on a horse-drawn cart. Reaching the cart, Dave knelt behind it.

The two men continued to leapfrog until they were two blocks away from the ambush.

Jogging down the dirt street, they looked for shelter, needing a few minutes to stop their leakers, catch their breath, and call in. They saw a partially opened wooden door on a ramshackle house. Without breaking stride, they kicked the door fully open and found themselves in the middle of a single-room dwelling.

The occupants froze in place at the sight of two armed giants exploding into their lives. Jax kicked the door shut, while Dave scanned the room for threats over his raised rifle. No guns were visible. The room had two windows, both cracked open, explaining the door being partially open in search of a cross breeze. The room had the noxious smell of a wood fire along with cooked sambusa and cardamom.

Dave put his finger to his lips. The four Somalis in the room, an elderly man, a younger woman, and two small kids all nodded their heads vigorously. Jax slid a heavy dresser in front of the door, hoping to buy them a second or two if someone tried to enter from the outside, and hoping to discourage his new hosts from fleeing. Once the room was secured, Dave strategically placed a chair that allowed him to observe the occupants, the windows, and the door.

He helped Jax remove his web-vest and shirt, and had him sit on the chair, leaning Jax's M4 against his leg for instant access. Jax was having trouble breathing and felt a little lightheaded; Dave could see why. The round that hit his arm must have hit the armored plate in Jax's vest and fragmented. A small piece of the bullet had entered Jax's chest and exited his back, creating a sucking chest wound. His right lung had collapsed from the external venting to the atmosphere. Without immediate aid, he could die.

As Dave was examining Jax, he noticed movement on the couch. He quickly drew his Glock from the holster on the front of his vest. The woman on the couch had her hands at chest level with her palms toward him, motioning that she was not a threat. Her family watched the two-person drama play out, afraid to move, afraid of the huge men with guns.

The woman moved slowly to the newly relocated dresser, never breaking eye contact with Dave. He tracked her with his pistol, aimed at the floor in front of her. He could have it on her in a tenth of a second. She pointed to the top drawer and raised her eyebrows in question. Dave nodded, not sure where this was going.

The woman opened the top drawer slowly. As she inserted her hand, Dave raised the pistol to point at her chest, his finger off the trigger, alongside the pistol frame. She retrieved a nurse's ID card from the drawer and held it up for Dave to read. It had a red caduceus snake and staff symbol, flanked by the red flag of Turkey and the blue flag of Somalia. Pointing at herself, Dave nodded again as he recognized the symbol for the Erdogan Hospital in the city.

He holstered his weapon as she placed her ID on the dresser.

Still watching Dave, the nurse approached Jax and began examining her new patient's wounds. Nodding in understanding, she circled through the tiny room, retrieving hydrogen peroxide, a porcelain dishpan, and some white cloths. After rinsing her hands in the hydrogen peroxide and drying them, she began to use a fresh peroxide-soaked cloth to clean the area around his entry and the exit wounds.

Dave opened Jax's trauma kit and removed two Asherman Chest Seals and a fourteen-gauge hypodermic needle. The nurse looked at the supplies and silently gave her approval.

Picking up one of the chest seals, she removed the backing from the adhesive and placed it over the wound on Jax's chest. She did the same for the exit wound on his back.

Jax's thorax had begun displacing due to the asymmetrical pressure against it in his chest cavity; that pressure had to be relieved. She palpitated his chest and inserted the needle between ribs at the second rib space, midclavicular line. They heard a pop and hiss of air as the pressure was released from Jax's chest cavity. His chest almost instantly returned to its normal shape. Relief washed over Jax's face as his breath came easier. The nurse removed the needle, holding the catheter in place and then capping it.

As Jax was putting his shirt back on, she pointed to Dave's arm where the bleeding had slowed to a steady ooze. Dave offered his arm to her. Using the trauma shears attached to the front of Dave's vest, she cut his sleeve up past the wound and pulled back the blood-soaked cloth to reveal a trough furrowed through his triceps, on the outside of his arm. The injury was not life-threatening, but it had to be covered. *An open wound is an invitation to get some obscure blood disease.*

Dave pulled an Israeli bandage from his own individual first aid kit, and handed it to the woman. Again, she used her white cloths and some hydrogen peroxide to clean the area around the wound. She poured the hydrogen peroxide directly into the cut and it stung and bubbled as it washed away the germs. Opening the sterile dressing and bandage combination, she applied it, securing it with the attached plastic clips. Dave's arm felt better just being bound. He nodded his thanks to her as she cleaned up the bloody rags. Jax was kitted up and guarding the door, showing no indication he had recently been shot in the chest.

Suddenly, everyone inside the house paused at the sounds of men shouting and running past. After half an hour, the excited voices and sounds of running died down. So far during this occupation of their home by the Americans, the other family members had remained silent as they sat on the couch.

At the top of the hour, Jax made whispered radio contact with the TOC. "Do you still have the backpack from the Hilux?" he asked Dave.

"Yes."

"Good. I put a ROVER in there. They're putting a Reaper on station for us."

Dave removed the ROVER and accessed the overhead video feed from the Reaper, giving him a God's eye view of his surrounding area.

Jax pressed the radio earpiece tighter in his ear as he received a message. He listened, then replied with three words, "Copy all. En route."

He looked at Dave and said, "We gotta go. Evac in fifteen mikes and we have six blocks to cover."

Dave nodded. He reached into the waistband of his jeans which held a tiny pouch hidden in the back. He inserted his finger into the pouch and pulled out a one-ounce bar of gold worth about thirteen hundred US dollars. That amount represented a year's salary in Somalia. Dave handed the small bar to the nurse.

"Mahadsanid," he said, 'thank-you' being one of the very few Somali words he knew. She closed her hand around the gold and nodded her head.

They moved out of the house and started down the street, with Dave using the ROVER to search his line of travel for any opposition. Seeing that no one was moving or congregating, they hugged the shadows of the buildings while moving cautiously toward their extraction point.

Jax was sluggish. His wound, combined with the heat and humidity, had taken more out of him than he let on. As they were moving past the closed door of an abandoned building, it opened. Two men and a young boy, all armed with AK-47s, stepped out of the door at exactly the same moment Dave and Jax were passing. There was no time for thinking.

All the technology and training in the world can't prevent happenstance.

"Gun!" was all Dave had time to yell as he turned and began firing, hitting the closest guy. Jax was a half-beat off his game. The second guy got off one round before Dave also shot him.

The kid was still fumbling with his rifle. Dave was justified in shooting him.

Eliminate everything that stands between you and escape, was the mantra.

But he didn't shoot. He moved his finger off the trigger and struck the kid in the chest using the end of his rifle barrel like a blunt spear. The blow knocked the kid on his ass, separating him from his weapon. Dave reached down, grabbed the AK-47, and threw it on top of the building. The kid cowered as Dave pointed his rifle at him. When he lowered his rifle, the kid scampered away.

Dave looked left and saw Jax sitting on the ground, his hands on his right thigh, blood pulsing between his fingers. With economy of motion, Dave pulled the CAT II tourniquet from Jax's web gear and, with a snap of his wrist, opened it into a loop large enough to fit over Jax's boot. He worked the tourniquet up past Jax's knee to the top of his thigh, above the wound. Dave began to wind the plastic stick, tightening the strap against his leg. Jax winced, but Dave quickly had the tourniquet tight enough to stop the flow of bright red blood. Jax was slipping into shock. The loss of blood from the earlier chest wound combined with the leg wound was devastating to his system. Dave had to get him medical attention—fast.

They were about two blocks from the extraction point and Dave was sure that the gunfire would attract more men with guns. They had to move. He slung Jax's weapon across his back and grabbed both of Jax's hands while facing him, like he was pulling him up to dance. Once Jax was standing, he leaned forward and allowed Jax to lay over his shoulders in a fireman's carry. Jax weighed 220 pounds and was wearing almost thirty pounds of battle gear. Dave hefted the additional 250 pounds and began fast-walking toward safety, carrying Jax the remaining distance without further contact. The kid must not have ratted them out . . . yet.

A flatbed truck was backed under a palm frond shelter and waiting for them at the extraction point. Before climbing onto the truck, Dave lowered Jax to the ground and removed a 500ml bag of Hextend plasma volume-expander from his backpack. He efficiently inserted an IV needle into one of Jax's antecubital fossa veins. Rolling the thumb wheel on the tubing started the flow of fluid that would buy Jax some time until he could receive proper medical treatment.

Before helping Dave to lift Jax onto the truck bed, the driver removed some floorboards, revealing a steel tray concealed beneath. They then lowered Jax into the hidden compartment. The tray was deep enough for both Jax and Dave to lie down with their gear placed at their feet. Dave held his rifle beside him in one hand and the plastic bag of IV fluid in the other. The driver replaced the wooden floorboards and placed lightweight boxes over the top of the boards to further camouflage the hide.

They made the forty-five-minute trip to the UN base at the airport without incident.

CHAPTER 4

The phone on Jackson Baer's desk in his DC office rang, interrupting his conversation. He checked the display and recognized the number. Holding up one finger to the man sitting across from him, he said, "I'm sorry, I need to take this." He picked up the phone and just said, "Hey."

The caller said, "Call me," and then hung up.

Jackson stood up from his desk, saying, "If you'll excuse me, I need to run out for a minute." He ushered the now insignificant man from his office.

Jax took the elevator down to the parking garage and walked quickly to his truck. He removed a burner from his glove box, walked to the edge of the parking structure to get better reception, and dialed one of the few numbers he knew from memory.

Dave answered; no pleasantries. "I've got a problem." As if they were back in the field, they defaulted to an economy of words.

More action, less talk.

"Okay."

"We need to meet. Soonest."

That statement implied there might be people involved who had the capability to trap their call, which in turn implied government involvement.

Dave was the most non-conspiratorial person Jax knew. He was usually the one people unknowingly referred to when they used the term, "*they*" do this, or "*they*" do that. He was "*that guy.*" So for Dave to be paranoid meant that some serious trouble was brewing.

"RP?" Jax asked, wanting to know the rally-point location to meet.

"Ready to copy?" Dave asked.

"Send it."

Dave recited in a monotone, "Blue-line local, add Tango Delta Lima Oscar Mikes from Castle at One, Six, Zero, Zero. How copy?"

"Lima Charlie," Jax acknowledged *loud and clear* before disconnecting the phone.

Jax quickly deciphered Dave's cryptic message.

Blue-line: mil-speak for a river; *Local*: nearby. The local river was the Potomac River.

Tango Delta, Lima Oscar,: *Terrorists Down, Last Operation* referred to the number of terrorists down or killed on their last operation, in Mogadishu. Body count, four.

Mikes or miles.

Castle referred to the White House.

Literal translation: Potomac River, add four miles from the White House at 1600 hours.

Four miles from the White House on the Potomac River at 1600 hours.

Jax returned to his truck and pulled a DC map from the center console. He used the scale across the bottom and noted where the four-mile mark on the river would place him: Fletcher's Cove Boathouse. He was to meet Dave there in two hours.

Jax called his administrative assistant on his regular phone. "Something's come up: a minor family crisis. Please cancel my appointments for today. I'll be back in the morning. Thanks." He had some things to do to get ready for tonight's meet.

His next call was to Efron Scott, who simply went by "Scott." The last person to call him "Efron" (other than his mother) might still be in a coma. Scott was a former Navy Seal. After five years as a tier two operator, he qualified for application to DEVGRU, an elite and secretive tier one arm of JSOC. He aced the training in the Green Team and he was selected, through an NFL-type draft, for the Red Squadron (Assault). His last five years had been spent in daily training interspersed with no-notice deployments to whatever operation the command staff decided was too risky or secretive for the regular military. Now retired, he owned a private security firm that advertised global protection for executives; however, his real job entailed supporting certain US government agencies' interests abroad.

Jax dialed; Scott answered.

"Scotty, you know who this is?" Jax asked.

"Yep."

"Can you meet me in thirty minutes?"

"Name the place."

They met at a Starbucks—nothing could be more benign than two "suits" meeting in the ubiquitous coffee shop. Jax ordered a regular black coffee. Scott ordered a grande white chocolate mocha with whip and two Sweet'n

Low, not exactly the stereotypical drink of a badass door-kicker and trigger-puller. They got their coffees and sat in the corner, away from the Wi-Fi leeches.

"You sounded a little stressed today. Everything okay?" asked Scott.

"You remember Dave Walsh?" Jax asked, without preamble.

"Sure. Quite a reputation. Some kind of super-spook. You two worked together back in the day, right?"

"Yeah, we did. He's got some kind of play going. I'm not sure what it is, but he wants to meet this afternoon, very discreetly."

"And you want my team to conduct a site survey and pull perimeter security, right?" asked Scott.

"Yep. The meet is at Fletcher's Cove Boathouse at 1600 hours. Can you put something together that quickly?"

"I've got a few guys in town I can chop over to this."

"Scott, this is on my nickel, not Uncle Sam's."

"No problem, I know you're good for it," Scott laughed. They worked out the details for the meeting and both left by different exits.

Scott and a three-man team arrived at the Boat House thirty minutes before the meet was scheduled, although his preference would have been to arrive two hours before to thoroughly scout their new AOR. He and his team had spent the preceding hour conducting pre-mission planning.

Since this was a non-government project, they utilized lower resolution Google Earth for their satellite imagery instead of the more powerful government satellites. Google Earth was effective enough to give them an overhead view of the meeting location and the surrounding areas. They were able to identify structures that any threats might use, sight lines to keep the principals in view at all times, and any potential, but hopefully not needed, fields of fire.

They determined routes of immediate ingress should they need to charge in like the cavalry, and routes of egress in case they had to get the hell out of Dodge. After everyone on the team spoke to their area of expertise, they marked the photos with red lines reflecting their intentions.

Two members of the security team set up positions allowing them observation of the only entry road. The third member of the team concealed himself in the tree line with a clear line of sight to the meet location. His laser range-finder showed 167 yards to the road entry point, his first probable point of interdiction.

A long, desert-brown, Cordura pouch lay unzipped on the grass beside him. The pouch contained his specialty tool, a Remington 700 BDL rifle modified with the H-S Precision box magazine, making it the civilian version of the Marine's M40A3 sniper weapon. He preferred the old school .308 caliber rifle with a Schmidt & Bender 3-12X50 PM II scope for ranges under 400 yards, and the AV/PVS-22 scope for night vision.

Non-snipers considered anything past 250 yards a long shot; he considered this "close in" work and preferred the Barrett .50 cal for the really long ranges. He kept the rifle in the bag, hoping he would not have to use it—things would have to go really badly to bring out that level of firepower in Washington, DC. He prepared his hide in the shadows, inserted his two-way radio earpiece, and conducted a comms check while scanning the area with high-powered binoculars.

Scott sat in his pick-up in the adjoining parking lot. With his team set and concealed, he called Jax. "All set. Overwatch in position; perimeter secure."

Jax simply replied with, "Copy."

At exactly 1600 hours, Jax pulled into the front parking lot of Fletcher's Cove Boathouse. His phone buzzed with an incoming text from Dave. "ARND BCK NR THE WTR."

Texting had been the death of vowels, Jax decided, as he looked at his phone.

He keyed his radio and spoke to Scott. "The meet's in the back. Moving now."

Scott replied, "We have eyes on."

Jax left his car and walked to the rear of the property overlooking the Potomac. As he rounded the corner of the building, he saw a line of canoes in almost every color in the crayon box. There, near the water, on a bench with a commanding view of the area, sat Dave and a young girl. Not being sure what to make of that, Jax stopped and scanned the area. Dave saw him and lifted his chin in greeting. Jax walked up and nodded.

Although he had not seen Dave in over six months, there was no embrace or long-lost bro handshake. He just sat on the end of the bench with Dave in the middle and the girl on the other end.

Dave said, "Security?"

Jax said, "Of course. Scotty, plus three."

"Good."

Jax looked over at the girl. She had her head down and was staring at the ground.

"Is it 'Bring Your Kid to Work' week?" Jax asked with a smile.

"This is Lydia," Dave answered. "Lydia, this is Jackson Baer."

"Hi, Lydia," Jax offered.

She looked up at the tall, trim man and offered a weak, "Hi."

Dave began the story: no embellishments, just a narrative. Pertinent facts in bullet form, just like a military briefing, which in a way, it was.

Jax listened intently to each detail as Dave gave him the maximum amount of information in the shortest amount of time. When Dave was finished, Jax asked, "Any idea who the strike team was?"

Dave shook his head. "No, but they were govies."

Lydia was now following the dialog intently.

Dave continued. "They likely killed the guy with the briefcase and would have done the same to the girl. They were cleaning up a problem."

Lydia gasped, put her face in her hands, and began to cry. Dave looked at Jax and shrugged. He started to put his hand on her shoulder, hovering close for a second, but then withdrew it without touching her. Lydia removed her hands from her face, and asked Dave, "Are they going to kill me?"

Dave looked at her for a minute before answering matter-of-factly. "No. I'm not going to let them."

"I can't go home, can I?" she asked, already knowing the answer.

"It would be best to let us sort this out first," Dave answered.

"Where do you live?" Jax asked.

"With friends. I'm in between jobs right now."

"Do you have family or friends in another city?"

"No," she said. "I've been on my own for four years."

Dave had already asked her those questions while they sat in his truck in the long-term parking lot at Dulles airport, waiting to meet Jax. The airport had open space and high-security entry control points, making it fairly safe from armed trackers.

Jax asked Dave, "Where's this USB drive now?"

"In my pocket."

"Have you seen what's on it?"

"No."

"I guess that's next—although I'm pretty sure we're not going to want to know."

"You're probably right."

"Let's go see the Wizard," Jax said.

As they stood up to leave, Jax reached behind his hip, removed a Sig P229 in a Kydex holster, and handed it to Dave. Dave secured the paddle holster on his belt, drew the weapon and pressed the magazine release button, dropping the mag in his hand, saw it was fully loaded, and re-inserted it. He racked the slide then press-checked it to see a round in the chamber. He activated the de-cocking lever to drop the hammer, and re-holstered it.

Jax touched the radio transmit button on the cuff of his shirt and keyed the bone-mic.

"How's it look?"

"You're clean," was Scotty's reply.

"We're relocating to the Wizard's. Collapse the perimeter. Can you guys stay on duty for a couple of hours?"

"Affirm," Scotty replied.

CHAPTER 5

The Wizard lived in a tough part of DC. Naylor Road was in the fourth district, where crime rates were as high as property values were low.

They parked along the curb in front of a small, gray, asbestos-sided house. The ancient, dark green roofing looked like it was melting and succumbing to gravity. The rusty chain-link fence surrounding the tiny lot had weeds growing through it. The yard was mostly dirt and the surviving clumps of grass had not been mowed in maybe ever. Scraggly trees littered the ground with their leaves and limbs.

Jax, in his vehicle, and Dave and Lydia in Dave's truck, waited for the "*all clear*" call from Scott. On Scott's signal, the three exited their vehicles and walked quickly to the front door with Jax leading, Lydia following in the middle, and Dave bringing up the rear. The two men instinctively reverted to their training by forming the protective bubble they utilized when escorting VIPs in high-threat environments.

The house had looked run-down from the street. Closer examination revealed windows and doors set in high-security steel frames; the dirt and grime had been carefully applied, like on a movie set. Jax removed a plastic RFID card from his pocket and held it up to a scanner concealed in the door frame. They heard a beep and a click as the door unlocked.

The interior of the house matched the exterior, with a shabby front entrance and threadbare carpet. The furniture was an eclectic mix of yard sale cast-offs. A trained eye would have been able detect the staging, as there was none of that old-house greasy smell and the walls were painted a smoke-stained shade of yellow, but there was no odor of ancient cigarette smoke.

"This place looks like a dump," Lydia said, the first unsolicited comment Dave had heard her make.

"Yes, it does!" Dave and Jax answered in unison, with a slight bit of pride.

"Let's go downstairs," Jax said.

A door leading off the kitchen hid stainless-steel elevator doors that he opened with another card swipe.

Lydia was now completely confused. "What is this place?" she asked.

"A communications center," Dave replied.

They stepped into the elevator. There were only two buttons. Jax pushed DOWN. The door closed with a *ding*, and Dave Brubeck's "Take Five" began playing over the elevator's speakers as if they were in a high-end department store. Dave and Jax looked at each other and shook their heads.

"No telling how much government time and money he spent getting music to play in this elevator," Jax said.

In exactly 2.4 seconds, they descended twenty feet underground.

The doors opened smoothly and they entered a dimly-lit room nicknamed, "The Dungeon." Nine, fifty-five-inch monitors mounted on the wall made a four-and-a-half-foot by fourteen-foot mega screen. An avalanche of information was pouring from them.

The "Wizard" was a twenty-three-year-old kid whose real name was Thomas Grant, a fact known possibly only to his parents and his security clearance investigator. Tall and lanky, complete with black frame glasses, he looked like a Hollywood extra who would run out from behind a curtain if the director yelled, "Send in the computer nerd!"

The Wiz sat behind a console of six keyboards linked to some of the fastest computers in the world. He'd begun his "career" as a computer hacker in middle school and was never caught until his "senior" year at George Washington University. In truth, he'd never attended a single college class, never paid a penny of tuition, and was never officially admitted to the university. In fact, he'd only been eighteen years old at the time but had managed to hack and socially engineer his entirely fictitious college career. If he hadn't been caught, he would have graduated, seen his picture in the university annual, and been on the dean's list.

His real hacking career and his fake college career both came to a screeching halt after a few celebratory beers had him believing that Serene, the cute blonde he was chatting up at the Merrymaker Bar, would be impressed with his exploits. As it turned out, her real name was Gretchen; Serene was her club name. She was a student at GW and reported the entire conversation to the dean of admissions, who found no humor whatsoever in the Wiz's play.

As luck would have it, the Wiz drew a very aggressive prosecutor whose self-worth was based on the size of the college degree his dad had bought for him. He was very eager to teach the young man a lesson. The judge gave young Mr. Grant a sentence of eleven months and twenty-nine days, the maximum allowable for a misdemeanor.

Uncle Sam found out about the kid from the dean's secretary, who happened to be married to the IT guy at a three-letter agency. The Wiz was intercepted before he was too far down the justice system's sewer. After spending a week in the DC Department of Corrections Jail on 14th Street, he was extremely willing to comply with his new handler's requests. They would tell him the information they needed and he was successful in fulfilling their desires. The Wiz was good—maybe even the best—which was why he enjoyed this setup instead of a six-foot by eight-foot jail cell with some illiterate redneck named Bubba.

The quantity and quality of the equipment at the comm center kept growing; the Wiz was in his element. He had an unlimited source of funding and equipment, and he loved his work. He could hack, cheat, and screw with whole countries and not only was it legal, but he got paid for doing it. In some circles, he was considered a national asset. Very few people knew the closely held secret of the Wiz and the Dungeon. Dave and Jax were two of the original stakeholders in establishing the requirements for this operation.

The Wiz spun around in his black office chair, looked up, scanned right past Dave and Jax, and said, "Who's the girl?"

Jax said, "It doesn't matter. We need you to look at something from a clean box."

The Wizard knew the drill. *Don't ask questions, just do it.*

The Wiz stood up and walked over to a cabinet, removing a laptop that had never been connected to an outside source or server. He took it into the faraday cage (the copper mesh enclosure that prevented electronic signals from entering or exiting) and powered it up.

Dave handed him the brass Cryptex vault. The Wizard turned it over in his hands as he examined it. "Way cool! It looks like something out of the Da Vinci Code." He began spinning the numbered dials, trying varying combinations. "This could take a while," he said as he continued trying various sequences.

Dave walked over to a red toolbox used for computer repairs and returned with a screwdriver. He held out his hand and the Wiz put the Cryptex in his palm. Dave used the Phillips screwdriver to unscrew the four small corner posts. The Cryptex vault fell apart on the table, the numbered wheels sliding off the brass housing. Dave picked up the USB drive that was now freed from the center of the brass tube and handed it to the Wiz. The younger man grinned and shrugged at the analog way in which Dave had solved a crypto problem.

Inserting the USB flash drive into the sterile laptop, the Wiz's hands flew over the keyboard as the screen filled with commands. "It's encrypted with some pretty serious codes, but I can break them. It should take a few hours . . . but give me ten minutes," Wiz said with a grin.

Jax and Dave moved around the room, watching cable news and satellite images. Lydia stayed very close to the Wizard, looking over his shoulder. After watching for a while, she asked, "Is it Symmetric-key Encrypted?"

41

The Wizard turned his chair around to look at her. "What do you know about Symmetric-key Encryption?"

"I know that if you don't have the key to the 128-bit AES encryption, you have a one-in-about 300-gazillian chance of breaking it," she answered.

"Well, that would be true, for mortals. Watch this," he said, as he stroked the keys.

Suddenly, a random pattern of letters and numbers populated the screen, scrolling down so fast that they looked like they were not moving. While the numbers and digits flowed, the Wizard asked, "Where did you learn about computers?"

Lydia replied, "I was kind of a loner in school; had plenty of time on my hands and something to prove. A guy friend of mine got me started in hacking, and I kind of took to it. Pretty soon, I was able to hack the school record system and change people's grades for lunch money. I got pretty good at it until I had to run."

"You mean, you ran away from home?"

"Yeah, when I was seventeen."

"Where do you stay?"

"Usually with friends. I'm trying to save up to get a place of my own. How about you?"

"Here. I live here in this building. I don't go out much and if I do, two guys with guns always go with me."

"That's gotta suck."

"It's not too bad. I get paid pretty well, and my bosses are pretty nice to me. Plus, I get any computer equipment I want."

"This is a sweet setup," she said, looking around at all the high-tech equipment.

"I've got to check on a program I've got running over there. I'll be right back."

Jax and Dave were in the small kitchen drinking coffee. "The girl seems pretty computer savvy," said Jax.

"Yeah, I heard," replied Dave.

"Maybe we could set her up here with the Wiz," Jax suggested.

"I'm not so sure about that. That's the first time I've seen him look interested in anything that doesn't have a keyboard," said Dave.

"Yeah, that's the most I've heard him say in the five years I've known him."

"Hey, where's Lydia?" Dave asked.

Jax looked in the comm center and didn't see either the Wiz or Lydia.

"Hey, Wiz!" Jax yelled.

"What?" the Wizard answered, from an adjoining room.

"Is Lydia back there?"

"Who?"

"The girl, Lydia."

"Well, if you had introduced her to me, I would have known who you were referring to," the Wizard said, and then added, "No, I thought she was with you."

Dave and Jax began moving at the same time. They ran to the elevator, but it had not been opened. The elevator needed a key-card to unlock it.

"The fire stairs!" Jax said.

Even clandestine government buildings had to meet fire codes, so the fire stairs had one-way doors. You could push your way out of the building, but there were no handles on the outside of the doors to gain entrance.

CHAPTER 6

Dave and Jax both ran to the stairs, climbing them two at a time. They pushed open the outside doors in time to see a black Suburban pull away from the curb and disappear down the street. Just as they headed toward their vehicles, two flash-bang grenades went off, surprising and deafening them. They stumbled and drew their weapons, but there was no one to shoot at. The flash-bangs had been set with an expedient trip wire to disorient the next person exiting the fire doors. This trick was hasty, but effective.

Jax, still deafened, heard a voice shouting in his earpiece. It was Scotty.

"Jax! Jax! I've been trying to call; we couldn't get you on the radio. We saw the Suburban pull up just as the girl walked out. We thought you sent a crew to pick her up. A guy bounced out of the SUV and grabbed her before we could get to her."

"Scotty, get some more security out here," Jax ordered, "and get your guys rolling! Find that SUV."

"We're on it!"

Smoke from the flash-bangs settled to the ground, saturating the air with the pungent smell of burnt potassium perchlorate.

"We're going back inside. I'll call you in ten minutes."

Dave looked down the street. He was building a scenario in his head, deciding who he was going to kill if they hurt her. *Hell, he might just kill them anyway.* He felt the familiar, pre-mission intensity building. But this wasn't a mission—or was it?

Dave sprinted toward the Dungeon. Jax ran to catch up.

***

Lydia had been a little flustered from her interaction with the guy they called the Wizard. He was cute enough, and he seemed really smart. She could tell that he knew a lot about computers.

Lydia knew a lot about them too, but she didn't let on. Most of the crowd she hung out with only owned a phone; they thought you were some kind of nerd if you knew about computers. She may or may not be a nerd, but she knew she was smart where it counted. It was easy to lose herself in computers—always finding new places to go, new puzzles to break, new things to look at, and no one to disappoint you. Her fingers took on a life of their own when she began hacking.

She'd begun feeling claustrophobic in the underground bunker and felt like she would suffocate if she didn't get outside. Seeing an exit sign, she'd followed it to the stairs that took her up and out of the building. Outside in the cool evening air, Lydia could breathe. Her mind raced as it tried to catch up with everything that had happened that day. Standing there with her eyes closed and her arms folded over her chest, she'd been thinking about running away from all this insanity.

Running always seemed to be her go-to plan.

Lydia had been startled and had screamed when a mountain of a man grabbed her from behind. His arms were rock hard and he smelled like stale sweat. Pinning her to his chest so tightly that she could barely breathe, he'd roughly pulled a black hood over her head. He clamped her mouth shut to stifle her screams and carried her off as if she weighed nothing.

She'd tried to fight and kick, but nothing seemed to faze the giant. Within seconds, she felt herself being pushed into a vehicle. She heard the door slam and the tires squeal, then two loud explosions echoed behind her as they raced away. Her arms were pulled behind her, and her wrists were tied with plastic zip ties. A blanket was thrown over her as she was pushed to the floor of the vehicle.

***

The Wizard was still working the flash drive when Dave and Jax entered the dark room. Numbers and symbols continued to scroll down the screen in an endless list. The Wizard kept clicking.

"What happened outside? What was that noise?" he asked, without taking his eyes off of the screen.

"They took the girl," Jax said.

"Who took the girl?" The Wizard's fingers froze over the keyboard while he met Jax's and Dave's eyes.

"We don't know yet. That's what we need you to tell us," Dave replied.

After about five minutes of tapping keys, the Wizard leaned back from the screen and said, "Okay, I've cracked the encryption." He brought his index finger in a large arc and dramatically hit the enter button. Within seconds of reading the data, his elation at breaking the code turned to shock.

"Ohhhhh, noooooo. This is not good, not good, not good, not good, no, no, no, no. This is so fucked," he stammered.

The screen had stopped scrolling and a spreadsheet was displayed on his monitor. Dave and Jax leaned in to read the information. The data looked like a summary sheet of mining and mineral rights in Iraq and Afghanistan. The contracts—lots of contracts—dated as far back as eleven years. In the far right-hand column, figures were posted labeled *Value.*

The total at the bottom of that column was over five hundred million dollars.

"Okay, Wiz, what's that mean?" Dave asked.

"It's not what . . . it's *who*," the Wizard said. "Look." He paged back to the previous screen and pointed. The names Warren Battles, Mike Davis, Allen Greensmith, and Foster Hillum were listed over and over on some type of banking statement.

The Wizard could clearly see the political nightmare unfolding in front of him, but Dave and Jax were just catching up. They wondered why the names of Dave's former boss, the Deputy Director of National Intelligence, Warren Battles, along with a retired three-star general, the current Secretary of Defense, and the CEO of one of the largest military equipment suppliers in the world would be on bank statements totaling millions of dollars.

Just then, the secure line in the Dungeon rang. The caller ID showed *DATA BLOCKED.* It was the first time the Wiz had seen his powerful caller ID defeated.

All three men looked at each other.

The Wizard picked up the phone like it was a rattle-snake. He didn't utter a word, just listened and then held the receiver out to Dave. "It's for you."

Jax looked at Dave with raised eyebrows and gave a little shrug.

Dave took the phone, and before the caller could say anything, he said, "If you hurt the girl, I'll kill you and everyone who works with you. Then I'll burn your houses to the ground. I'll find who hired you and I'll kill them too. I'm talking scorched earth."

"Calm down, the girl's fine," the caller said. "If you want her to stay that way, give me the USB drive, without reading it. You haven't read it, have you?"

"No," lied Dave. "What's on it?"

"Nothing of interest to you. Bring it to Tyson's Corner Mall at 1600 hours tomorrow. I'll have the girl there," the caller said, and hung up.

Dave struggled to understand this new paradigm.

He had been in many life-and-death situations, but he'd always known who the good guys were and who the bad guys were, a knowledge that gave Dave clarity of mission and allowed him to sleep at night. He was on the side of righteousness.

Warren Battles had been a part of several of Dave's operations over the years. He had leveraged the success of those operations to work his way to the top of the political food chain and had been named the DDNI four years ago. Warren was one of the few people Dave trusted.

This evidence, pointing to his involvement in some kind of conspiracy, was beyond belief. Dave felt his whole world shift under his feet.

He looked at his watch; they had very little time to review the data on the thumb drive, find who took Lydia, and develop a plan to rescue her. Both he and Jax knew that the people who took her had no intention of letting her live; they also knew that the kidnappers would attempt to kill Dave and Jax.

That would be a little tougher.

As Dave and Jax were leaving the underground lair, Jax stopped just before stepping into the elevator. He motioned with his head for Wiz to come over.

"I want you to access those accounts, right now, and here's what I want you to do . . .."

CHAPTER 7

Other than manhandling her into and out of the SUV, they had not hurt her. Lydia's fear was now turning to anger.

They had deposited her in a small, windowless, locked room. It had a twin bed, a chair in front of a desk, and lights recessed in the ceiling. There were no sheets or blankets on the bed, and every piece of furniture was bolted to the floor. There wasn't even a light switch. The room reminded her of the juvie cells where she had spent more than a few nights in her youth.

That big guy she'd met on the bench, Dave, said that he wouldn't let anything happen to her . . . yet this was so typical of her life. Everyone was full of promises, but very few delivered.

She began the process of acclimating—that's what you did when bounced from institution to institution, foster home to foster home; you acclimated and learned how to blend in with your most recent environment. Early on, she'd bought plenty of lessons in failing to blend in. Failing to blend in made you a target—a target for bullies and perverts. Becoming the object of their attention always led to pain of some sort. Once you blended in, you could escape. It was always her goal to get away. But before you could blend in, you had to find the boundaries. That would be Lydia's first task.

Exhausted from adrenaline and fear, she slept fitfully for several hours. The ceiling light, constantly illuminated, skewed her sense of time. She woke up with a sour taste in her mouth and foul breath. Still wearing the blood-stained dress from yesterday, she felt grimy. And she really had to pee.

Despite her discomfort, she began formulating an escape plan. It began with pounding on the door. "Hey! I gotta pee! Anybody out there?" she yelled. Not hearing anyone, she yelled again, "Hey! Are you there?" In a moment, she heard a key being fitted into the lock.

The door swung open soundlessly revealing a short, stocky woman standing in the doorway. She had mousy brown hair and no makeup; she wore a white shirt with a navy blue blazer and mid-calf skirt. "What?" she asked.

"I gotta pee, and I'm hungry."

"I'll bring you breakfast. Don't yell like that. Just knock on the door and I'll come and check on you."

"I need to go to the bathroom. Where am I? Who are you? Why did you take me?" Lydia blurted out.

CHAPTER 8

Warren Battles sat alone in his huge corner office, looking out over the nation's capital. His mahogany desk, the size of a small car, was cleared and organized like a demonstration poster for OCD.

He felt something he had never experienced in his long career of operating in the dark underbelly of clandestine politics.

Fear.

His security lead had just called.

Somehow, one of their low-level data crunchers had copied information and smuggled it out of the building. They were unclear as to motive, and more importantly, what information was contained on the USB drive.

Warren Battles was at the pinnacle of his career, and his rise to the role of world's top operational spy-master had sometimes been like a running gun battle. *Take shots when you can and keep moving.* As Principal Deputy Director, National Intelligence, he served in a role similar to that of a Chief Operating Officer. His focus was on the operations of the Office of the Director of National Intelligence.

The position was perfect for him. He let his boss, the DNI, take all the political and public stones that were hurled while he quietly operated with impunity in the shadows. His charge was to thwart attacks on his country, but he also had to maintain a constant vigilance for internal political raiders seeking to unseat him.

It was a two-front war and he was better at fighting political battles than he was at suppressing threats to the homeland. He had made the political fights his priority. The two maxims he clung to were power and control; they fed each other. The cold tendril of fear he felt at the moment was that of discovery—discovery of black deeds done in secrecy; discovery that his actions of self-interest compromised the national security he had sworn to protect.

Battles had found a fertile incubator for his particular kind of sociopathic narcissism in the air force, where he'd always felt like he was the grown-up amongst a group of teenagers. Nothing was sacred to him and he was intelligent enough to never get caught in the web of lies and deceit he cast. He still chuckled at how he'd grabbed the top cadet position at the Air Force Academy—for him, it had been easy. The selection process had been tight, and he was clearly in second position.

One night, he'd gone off base to an adult bookstore and removed several of the mail-in subscription cards from some of the raunchiest porn magazines, filling in the leading candidate's name and academy address and mailing them off with cash. Soon, an endless stream of porn magazines began arriving at the base post office addressed to his competitor. End of competition.

Battles prevailed in the selection process, and also learned a valuable life lesson.

Dirty tricks among men of honor work most of the time.

Warren continuously fine-tuned his skills of deception throughout his career and had yet to be discovered. After garnering outstanding fitness reports from his commanding officer at his last military posting, he was truly the epitome of a wolf in sheep's clothing. It helped that he had photos of his commanding officer drinking with a prostitute—a prostitute that Battles happened to hire . . . along with the photographer.

Battles felt he was simply the smartest person in the room, no matter the setting. After all, this was his movie of life and everyone else was just an extra.

One of the keys to his success was that most people underestimated him, or at least underestimated his ruthlessness. Usually, it was because they refused to believe anyone could be that evil—until it was too late. His learned social mannerisms along with his stately appearance and quick smile worked like a cloaking device to hide his true intentions, and a nagging insecurity drove a relentless need to succeed. For him, it was never good enough to just win; anyone who opposed him had to lose, and lose big-time.

His opposition was anyone he perceived to have slighted him, challenged him, or dared to disagree with him. Most of the time, he was a smooth operator. He reserved his volatile screaming fits for those closest to him and always behind closed doors. For Battles, a master of manipulation, there were no rules except his own.

"Linda! Get Senator Jameson on the phone for me!" Battles yelled from his office. He had an intercom, but he liked to bark orders across the room. His communication style served to remind the troops who was in charge.

"Yes, sir!" the awestruck assistant replied. His entire staff was awestruck because he fired them as soon as they weren't.

"Mr. Battles, I have the senator on the line," Linda announced in her best professional voice over his intercom.

"Senator, how are you?" Battles cooed to the Chairman of the US Senate Armed Services Committee.

"Great, Deputy Director, and you?" the senator replied.

"I'm well. And how are Barb and the kids?" Battles asked, making the expected social inquiry about his wife and children.

"Well, they're great too. Daniel is in England for a semester, and little David is—" the senator was abruptly interrupted.

"And how's Janine?" Battles asked, making the unexpected and unsociable inquiry about the senator's mistress.

"What do you want, Warren?" the senator asked, all pretense of civility gone from his voice.

"Now David . . . don't get testy with me. I would like for you to review a recommendation for a pending medal on the books for that kid from Alabama," Battles replied.

"The Silver Star we are going to award Jason Albertson? What about it? The kid is a hero," the senator replied.

"That may well be, but we are not going to reward the senator from Alabama who opposed my budget proposal last August," Battles stated firmly.

"Warren, what does Senator Michaels have to do with Jason Albertson saving the lives of three of his teammates, while wounded and under fire in Afghanistan?" the now flustered senator asked.

"The young soldier had the misfortune of being from Alabama. I will not give the good senator from Alabama one second of national television to crow about himself or the state of Alabama. Pull back the medal," Battles demanded before he slammed down the phone.

CHAPTER 9

The four men sat around the dark mahogany conference table in the small meeting room at the Army-Navy Club in Arlington. They were leaning in, paying careful attention to the dialogue, as if their careers, and possibly their lives, depended on it.

"What was on the thumb drive?" Battles asked retired General Mike Davis.

"Our IT guys are still trying to determine exactly what Mark Burris copied from his workstation. They are trying to determine how he accessed the secure shared drive that was partitioned off for our use only. They say they'll have that information in less than four hours."

Davis hadn't earned his third star by speculating; he was known for his precision and his ruthlessness to succeed at anyone's expense, particularly his staff's.

"Where's the thumb drive right now?" Battles demanded from Davis.

"We're working that as well. Fortunately, Burris used his company-issued briefcase to get the thumb drive out of the building. Our people can only use company-issued briefcases, and unknown to them, they all contain RF trackers. IT security discovered the data breach within minutes. Our Watchdog Program was triggered when he wrote to his thumb drive port from the classified computer.

"Burris cleared the security checkpoint utilizing a forged classified courier letter to walk the briefcase out. He was on the street by the time our security team arrived. But one of our plainclothes guys saw him about a block away and started chasing him on foot. This was all going down in the middle of the day with lots of people around, so our security guy pulled his knife instead of his gun. When he grabbed Burris from the back, Burris turned and hit our security guy in the head with the briefcase. Our guy panicked and stabbed him. It must have looked like a street mugging because some overzealous citizen intervened, tackled our guy, and gave Burris the chance to run off."

Davis continued. "The rest of the team got there within five minutes. They found Burris about two blocks away on the sidewalk, face-down, dead. He'd bled out and the briefcase was gone. We called out a striker team and set up a perimeter within minutes. We initially thought Burris met a contact and handed the briefcase off, but that didn't seem likely—his escape was too rushed, too unplanned. We eventually found that he'd handed the briefcase to some random girl on the street. She was seen running away from Burris, but initially, our guys didn't spot the briefcase. Later, we saw her with an older man, sitting on a park bench. Before we could get to her, they walked away. We lost them but reacquired them with the RF tracker. The case was recovered but the drive had been removed."

"Who was the girl?" Battles asked.

"Unknown at this time. We think she's random; we think she's unwitting," Davis answered.

"Who was the man?" Battles demanded.

Fear flickered across General Davis's face.

"Dave Walsh. We pulled the tape from an ATM security camera across the street from the café where we recovered the briefcase. One of our analysts recognized him going in with the girl."

Except for Foster Hillum, every man in the room knew about the legendary exploits of Dave Walsh.

"How's Walsh involved in this?" Secretary of Defense Greensmith asked.

"We think it's completely accidental," Davis answered.

"Warren, he works for you. Call him and tell him to give the drive back," the SecDef demanded.

"He worked for me, as in past tense. He retired six months ago."

"There's more," Davis interjected. Heads turned toward him like zebras watching a lion approach their herd. "Walsh's truck was ID'd and we were able to track it using overhead assets. We found the girl outside a black-ops comm center located in a residential area. We grabbed her, thinking she might have the drive. She didn't. We called Walsh and told him we wanted the drive."

"What did he say?" asked Greensmith.

"He told us to bring the girl back," Davis replied, without the emotion that was screaming inside of him.

"Will he come after her?" asked the SecDef.

General Davis paused as he made and held eye contact with the Secretary of Defense.

"Sir, he will come after her," he paused again to make sure his boss did not miss the next part, "and us. He is relentless, ruthless, well trained, and experienced. We do not want to go to war with this guy."

"Bullshit!" Battles spat. "He's a man; he can die. If we don't get our drive back, that's exactly what he will do: die. If not, we'll all go to federal prison for a very long time."

The room was deathly quiet.

"It may not be that simple," General Davis replied.

"He is well-respected by the DNI and the president. Anything that happens to Walsh will get POTUS's attention. The heat will be unbearable."

"General, this is your mess. Unfuck this as quickly and quietly as possible. Get that drive and whatever information's on it back. Use whatever resources or force necessary. Do I make myself clear?"

"Crystal, sir."

CHAPTER 10

Halfway down the drive to his house, Dave hit the garage door opener on his sun visor. He had timed it so that the garage door opened fully just as he rolled into the space. The ceiling-mounted laser placed a red dot on his dash, showing him exactly where to stop. He pushed the button again, and the door closed as he turned off the ignition.

He sat behind the wheel for a minute trying to sort out the day's events.

Why had he become involved with the girl on the bench?

She was an innocent. She was unwitting.

He knew if he hadn't gotten involved, she would not have survived an encounter with the owners of that briefcase. Besides, it was the right thing to do.

The right thing to do.

How many times had he done the *right thing* for his country, at the direction of Warren Battles, the man whose name was on those documents on the thumb drive? Had he been used by his own government? Was he that blinded with patriotism?

He disarmed the alarm system as he entered the house and pushed play on his Bose entertainment system. Richard Elliot's soft saxophone riffs filled the room.

He dropped his keys on the countertop.

The kitchen was his favorite room in the house. He had many fond childhood memories of spending time with his Italian mother as she taught him to cook. He utilized those skills primarily for survival, until later in life when the art and techniques of cooking caught his attention. Now he enjoyed the process, the science and the art of it. He found he loved creating dishes that were as appealing visually as they were delicious.

He wondered if a life spent destroying things could be atoned for by creating things. It was quite a dichotomy. His warrior compatriots respected one of their own who could create with the same skill that they could destroy, whether it was writing, cooking, music, or art.

He'd bought the colonial style house and farm in rural Virginia several years ago using money from his deployment premiums. The government paid its employees fairly well for risking their lives. An uncle, also a stockbroker, helped him invest wisely. Not having a family to support and being constantly deployed, his money grew exponentially.

Dave had remodeled the old house with an emphasis on a state-of-the-art kitchen. A red Bertazzoni six-burner gas range with a convection oven anchored the kitchen space. A stainless-steel Sub-Zero refrigerator and a huge stainless-steel sink completed the efficient work triangle. Marble countertops and a large marble island provided plenty of prep space. He leaned against the counter as he gazed out the window over the sink. The tranquil scenery and seclusion that usually provided respite now conflicted with his emotions.

Dave felt the familiar dark shadow of depression begin to wrap its tendrils around him and creep up the back of his neck. This was how the low-intensity headaches leading to full-blown migraines within hours always began. He closed his eyes tightly, squeezing them hard, trying to blot out the light in an attempt to stave off the inevitable.

He dropped into one of the kitchen chairs, the scene that brought on these episodes playing in an endless loop in his head.

His wife and child, dead.

Him, helpless to prevent it.

He visualized the horrific crash that had taken their lives. One minute, they were alive and vibrant; the next instant, nothing—just blackness. They never had a chance.

A drunk driver had slammed into them at over fifty miles an hour. Dave should have been there for them. He should have been driving. He could have avoided the crash, or so he told himself over and over. Instead, the two he loved most were killed. The drunk driver survived.

Dave placed his head on the kitchen table, closed his eyes, and drifted off into a fitful sleep.

***

An hour later, the buzzing of his phone vibrating on the table, woke him.

The caller ID said UNKNOWN. He pushed the green button and brought the phone to his ear, but he didn't say anything. An electronically synthesized voice said, "Give us back the drive."

"Where is she?"

"She's safe. We just want the USB drive."

"You are going to die, that's a given. If she is harmed, everyone who had a part in this, or even thought about this, will die. You've got one hour to drop her off in front of the house where you took her," Dave said evenly without a trace of emotion, but with finality.

The caller disconnected without responding.

Dave's phone had a few features normal phones didn't have. He was able to record the conversation and trap the physical location of the call, but he needed help to process the information for details. He dialed the Wizard.

The Wizard answered, "Go."

"Sending data for tracking and analysis. This one showed up as UNKNOWN instead of DATA BLOCKED. I think they used a different phone," Dave said, not needing to identify himself.

"Send it."

"Call me back soonest."

"Copy."

Dave hung up and headed to the garage behind his house.

The two-car garage housed two restoration projects he had completed between deployments: a cream-colored 1952 MG TD and a Fiesta Red 1956 Ford Thunderbird. The frame-off restorations had each taken years to complete due to his deployment schedule. He used to put the top down and drive to the delightful screams of his daughter while her long blonde hair streamed in the wind.

Now he kept them covered. Neither car had been moved since the crash. That was eight years ago.

Unbeknownst to Dave, his housekeeper, Miranda, had her brother come over once a month and check the tire pressures and start the cars to keep the batteries charged. She knew how much the cars meant to Dave and his family and felt an obligation to take care of him.

What she didn't know was that Dave planned to give Miranda's daughter her choice of one of the cars as a gift when she graduated from college.

The value of either of the cars, if sold, would offset about two years of college loans.

Dave walked past the cars to the back wall. There he opened one of the lower cabinet doors, reached in, and punched a code on a hidden keypad. The code allowed one of the metal cabinets lining the back wall to swing open, revealing a door to a hidden room with a cipher lock on it. He dialed the combo and pulled the door open.

After switching on the fluorescent lights in the room, he disarmed the alarm system. The lights blinked to full power, illuminating an array of weapons that would be the envy of any small police department's SWAT team.

Dave started gathering the gear he would need, including a black armored vest, an M4 rifle, a Glock 19, six flash-bang grenades, 2 tear gas grenades, 2 white smoke grenades, 1 thermite grenade, his Night Vision Devices, and a Cold Steel fighting knife. He dropped the gear into a large Under Armour equipment bag, slung his armored vest and M4 over his shoulder, and secured the room before returning to his truck.

Raising the Leer fiberglass tonneau cover on the bed of his truck and lowering the tailgate, he accessed the TruckVault that was built into the truck. Keying in the combos, he opened the two long drawers and pushed the equipment bag into one, his vest and M4 in the other, and locked them back.

He backed out of the drive and headed for the Wizard's lair.

CHAPTER 11

As he drove, he passed a small cemetery and a memory leaked out of one of the many tightly sealed compartments in his brain. The memory of another cemetery on a spring day, a few years past, was like acid leaking from an old battery and just as corrosive.

Springtime in Virginia usually promises renewed life, but not this springtime. Raindrops slowly but steadily leak from the gray clouds, mingling with the mourner's tears.

The first time Dave Walsh sees the two headstones planted side by side with the names Laura Walsh and Sarah Walsh, his wife and daughter, he falls to his knees. The lush green grass had almost healed itself from where it was ripped open, allowing people he didn't know to place his family in the ground.

He was supposed to protect them, but he had failed. Instead, he had been on a mission eight thousand miles away, doing the honorable thing, protecting his country and his family. He had succeeded at his mission, but failed his family.

Dave had never cried. Now he sobbed.

He had seldom loved. Now he grieved.

At fourteen, Sarah was just becoming a woman—smart, beautiful, and funny. She had her mom's good looks and humor, and her dad's insight and resourcefulness.

Laura and Sarah represented everything right in the world. He constantly marveled at how alike they were: beautiful in mind, spirit, and body. Every moment with them was pure joy. Now, they were gone.

CHAPTER 12

The short, stern woman—Lydia had begun thinking of as her prison guard—was holding a yellow Taser in her hand. "These hurt like a bitch and will knock you on your ass. I'll shoot you with this if you try to run."

Lydia nodded, her mind racing, as she looked for a means to escape.

The woman pointed down a hall. Lydia walked toward the bathroom.

"Don't close the door," the woman instructed.

"What? Are you hoping to cop a look? Do young girls turn you on?" Lydia shot back, deliberately baiting her captor, looking for an emotional advantage over her.

"Shut up and do your business."

Lydia took in her surroundings. She was determined to memorize every window, door, and attic access in order to find a way out. She also listened for any noises from inside or outside her prison that would give her a clue as to where she was being held.

"Hey, there's no toilet paper in here," Lydia yelled, lying and trying to lure her captor into the small space.

"Use your hand," the stern woman yelled back.

Lydia thought, *I have two options. I can distract her and try to escape, or I can overpower her.*

That damn Taser was going to be a problem.

It was then that she saw the shower curtain. *Maybe there's a way . . ..*

"Are you finished?" the woman asked.

Lydia didn't answer. She slammed the bathroom door shut and locked it. The woman fished the key out of her pocket, unlocked the door, and then pushed the door partially open with her foot, but she couldn't see the girl.

She extended the Taser in front of her and entered the bathroom.

Just as the door fully opened, she saw Lydia. She was wrapped up in something.

About the time the woman realized what the girl was wrapped in, she'd already pulled the trigger on the Taser.

Two electrically charged barbs attached to thin wires shot into the plastic shower curtain Lydia had wrapped around her torso.

The last thing the woman saw was the white blur of the ceramic toilet top as Lydia swung like A-Rod driving one to the fence. The tank lid and the woman's head connected with a sickening *thud* and a splash of bright red hit the wall behind her. She collapsed without uttering a sound.

Lydia dropped the heavy top and shrugged off the shower curtain. She was afraid to touch the two thin wires still attached to the end of the Taser and embedded in her make-shift plastic armor. She searched the unconscious woman for keys, but found them still in the lock of the bathroom door.

Lydia moved slowly and purposefully to the front door while watching for other guards.

She looked through the peephole to see if anyone was guarding the front door. Not seeing anyone, she unlocked the dead bolt and stepped outside.

She had been held in an ordinary house in an ordinary neighborhood.

Hiding in plain sight, she had once heard someone say. No one would suspect that a hostage was being held here.

Lydia quickly moved away from the house and onto the sidewalk. As she headed toward the intersection, she scanned for guards in parked cars; none were evident. She could hear the traffic on the freeway and began moving in that direction. She needed to hitch a ride back to the Wizard's place.

But what she really needed was that guy Dave to come and get her.

CHAPTER 13

Despite his constant deployments to filthy areas around the world, Dave was a neat freak.

Maybe it was a way of exerting some control over his life of near chaos. Also, his constant travel required him to have some assistance with the house.

Miranda Sanchez had proven to be a lifesaver. She had helped his wife, Laura, and now did the same for Dave by coming in one day a week to clean. For years, she had been like a part of the family.

When he had been at home, Dave had enjoyed over-hearing Laura and Miranda talk. They covered lots of different topics like two old friends, but there was always one recurring theme: Miranda's daughter, Selma. Miranda was a single mom.

Her daughter was the center of her universe.

***

Miranda was watching the clock and thinking about her daughter Selma's graduation tonight. She had worked hard to put her through school. That night, Selma would be the first of the Sanchez family to ever graduate from college; that thought made Miranda's heart swell with pride.

Miranda had slowly built her house cleaning business to the point that she now had two customers each day. She always started early and worked late, giving each job the attention to detail that she would want for herself. That quality endeared her to her customers, many of whom knew she had a daughter in college, and had, on occasion, given money toward Selma's school expenses.

Miranda was so distracted by thoughts of the coming evening that she barely heard the knock at Dave's back door.

As she walked through the kitchen, she could see a man in a brown uniform at the door holding a cardboard box. She thought it was strange that a delivery man would walk all the way around the house and not use the front door. She would tell this delivery man to use the front door from now on.

She opened the door to a young, muscular man, his brown ball cap pulled down to shield his eyes. Before she could utter a word, he advanced through the doorway, holding the box in front of him and forcing Miranda to back up. As she started to protest, he dropped the box and fired three silenced .22 caliber rounds into Miranda Sanchez's forehead.

The killer stopped and listened for signs of anyone else in the house. As he moved back toward the door, he was careful not to step in the blood that was slowly pooling in a crimson halo around her head. Miranda lay inert on the kitchen floor she had so fastidiously cleaned just minutes ago. Her once sparkling eyes, only seconds ago rejoicing in her daughter's success, were now lifeless and open, staring at nothingness.

The gunman walked to the corner of the house, looked to see if any neighbors were in sight, and motioned to the driver of the truck to pull up the drive. Three men exited the back of the truck, walked between the truck and the house to remain out of sight, and quickly entered the house. The driver backed out of the driveway and drove to the preplanned holding area, a local rental storage lot about a half-mile away.

The killer motioned to two of his accomplices and they quickly found a bathroom, returning with three large bath towels. They wrapped her head with one, used another to quickly wipe up most of the blood on the floor, and laid the third over the remaining blood so that they wouldn't leave bloody footprints. Then they took the body to that same bathroom and unceremoniously dumped it into the bathtub.

The three men spread out through Dave's house, methodically searching it while the shooter kept a watch on the street.

A USB drive is very small and could be hidden almost anywhere. They tore through his office, bedroom, kitchen, and even the bathrooms with no sign of the device. They checked every obvious, and some not-so-obvious places, except for the base of one of the lamps in the living room. Dave had pulled back the fabric covering that base and inserted the USB into the stem of the lamp. He'd then glued the fabric back in place.

After two hours of searching, the team leader gave a small whistle. The three men met him in the kitchen, all shaking their heads.

"Just got a call from the driver. Someone's inbound. The driver is on the way to pick us up," the lead said. He pulled out his cell phone and called his boss. "We didn't find anything; we've been searching for two hours. Somebody is headed this way." After listening for a few seconds, he replied with, "Copy, wilco."

"Let's go," he said to his team.

Before leaving through the kitchen door, he pulled the huge red stove away from the wall and ripped the flexible gas line from the back of the stove. Gas flowed freely into the house. He reached into his jacket pocket and removed a small plastic box that had one switch, one LED light, and a wire antenna wrapped around the box. Unwrapping the thin wire antenna, he slid the power switch up. The red LED illuminated.

He sat the box on the counter and walked out the door. As the van drove away, the shooter very precisely dialed a number and pushed *send*. Within seconds, Dave's house erupted into a huge orange fireball.

The text to his boss simply said: *Done*.

CHAPTER 14

Lydia needed to find the house with the comm center in the basement.

She walked about two blocks toward the freeway entrance and saw a Starbucks on the access road. She buttoned Dave's blue windbreaker over her dirty dress and walked into the coffee shop. She had no money, no phone, hair that hadn't been combed in two days, and little time before the gorillas who abducted her would begin searching for her.

She headed to the back of the coffee shop and sat at a table next to a college-aged guy.

Smiling, Lydia began to spin a pretty good sob story about how her car and computer were stolen, and that she had to complete a job application that day. She sidled over to his table saying, "Do you mind?" and without waiting for an answer, moved his computer in front of her.

Her fingers rapidly pounded the keys—no finesse, just efficient, rapid keystrokes trying to sync the output of her hands with the idea developing like an explosion in her brain.

Her first venture off the digital straight-and-narrow had been as a script kiddie, using pre-built programs to hack into relatively benign databases, such as her high school grading system. As her skills sharpened, she became a full-fledged cracker; with the right equipment, there were very few systems she could not hack.

Lydia's finesse and attention to the subtleties of the systems she hacked made her more adept than most of the male crackers she knew who used brute force to break into databases.

She liked to sneak in and tiptoe around, leaving no trace when she left. Lydia thought of herself as a gray hat, hacking for the sport of it, not for financial gain or maliciousness, although she had dropped a little malware on a couple of jerk-off former boyfriends. It had taken them months to get back online after the little surprises she left on their system. Some were still getting twenty ads a day for penis enlargement; they never figured out who was responsible.

Lydia was envious of the Wizard's setup. That was some sweet equipment. She wished desperately that she had access to his equipment now.

Ignoring the college guy's confused stare, Lydia turned his laptop screen away from him and began searching every federal database, trying to find Dave Walsh. He was a wraith: there was absolutely nothing out there on him. After about ten minutes, she switched to trying to find Jax and was able to find limited information on Jackson Baer. Digging deeper, she found his cell phone number and address in the power company's database. With the ability to memorize almost anything, Lydia entrenched Jax's contact information in her brain.

Dumping her search history, Lydia turned the laptop back to the young man. With a disarming smile she asked, "Do you mind if I use your cell phone for one call?"

He had watched in awe at her keyboarding skills, as he'd never seen anyone type that fast. He had no way of knowing that the average person types at about 50 words per minute, whereas Lydia managed close to 200 words per minute.

"Uh, sure," was all he could muster, as he extended his iPhone to her.

She dialed the number she had just discovered. Jax answered on the first ring.

"Hello?"

"Hey, it's me. Your friend's friend," she said, as she turned away from her newfound source of tech equipment.

"Where are you?"

"I'm at a Starbucks on"—she looked out the window for the street sign—Wisconsin Avenue Northwest."

"Tenleytown," the college boy added.

"What?" Lydia asked.

"Tenleytown; you're in Tenleytown."

"I'm in Tenleytown," Lydia said to Jax while she smiled and winked at the college boy.

"Don't move from there. Do not leave with anyone unless they tell you the name of the young man Dave and I took you to meet the other day."

"Okay."

She hung up and handed the phone back to the young man. "Thank you."

"Uh, you're welcome. That seemed pretty serious."

"Just some family drama." She smiled.

He smiled back. She knew it would be good if he stayed with her until her ride showed up. Sitting with him would help her blend in, and it might give her a chance to run if the goons who took her showed up first. She kept a close eye on the doors and the parking lot.

The boy kept smiling at her. Her hair was a rat's nest and her breath smelled bad, but guys tended to overlook all that—especially horny guys. She maintained eye contact and smiled just enough to keep his interest, occasionally touching his hand. She had lived on her own long enough to know almost all the tricks of the streets.

"What's your name?" he asked.

"Jane. Jane Meacham," she lied, giving one of her high school classmate's names. She couldn't stand Jane Meacham. She had been a cheerleader and a snob. But it was the first name that popped into her head.

"I'm Daniel Roe," he said, as he extended his hand. She took his hand and shook it firmly. "Don't you need to call the police or something?"

Lydia looked at him strangely.

"About your car being stolen," Daniel said.

"Oh, yes, that! Yes, I do. I must be in shock."

He handed his phone back to her.

Lydia faked dialing the number as well as an entire three-minute phone call with the police department, going into great detail about the make, model, and color of her nonexistent car.

After her role-playing, she handed the phone back to Daniel. "Thanks again. They're on their way," she said.

"No problem. Do you want me to wait till they get here?"

"Sure, that would be great."

He chatted about his school, and she made up stuff about her school.

She was very believable.

CHAPTER 15

The phone ringing through his truck's sound system broke Dave's waking nightmare. The caller ID showed it was the Fairfax County Sheriff's office.

"Is this Mr. James Simpkins?" the caller asked.

Dave could hear the radio calls in the background, so he knew it was a police dispatcher.

"Yes," Dave answered.

Interesting, he thought. *That's the name I used to register my house and land.*

"This is the Fairfax County Sheriff's Office. You need to go to your house. There has been some trouble there and our deputy needs to talk to you."

"What kind of trouble?"

"Sir, I'm not at liberty to say. They just need your presence there."

"Okay. I'm on my way. I'm about an hour out," Dave replied, as he turned his truck around. As soon as the dispatcher disconnected, Dave called a guy he'd gotten to know from the shooting range.

"Dayton," the Fairfax County Sheriff answered his personal cell phone. He was all business today.

"Tom, it's Dave. I just got a call from your office that there's some trouble at my house."

"Ah—shit, Dave. Yeah, your house burned. It looks like a natural gas fire that started in the kitchen."

"Are you there now?"

"Yes."

"How bad?"

"Pretty bad. Most of the back of the house is gone. A neighbor called it in about the time your fire alarm went off."

"Tom, is there an old Chevy Nova in the drive?"

"Uh, yes there is."

"Tom, is my housekeeper Miranda Sanchez there?"

"I haven't seen her, and I was the second car on the scene. Ah, damn it. We'll do a full sweep of the house. The fire's been knocked down, but they're still putting water on it. Are you in the country?"

"Yes. I'm about fifty-five minutes out."

"Okay. Drive safely. I'll see you when you get here."

Dave pulled over and opened his TrunkVault. He rifled through a card file and pulled out a driver's license in the name of James Simpkins, just in case. It was a valid Virginia driver's license under a fictitious name.

He wasn't worried about the sheriff; Tom Dayton had been part of the Special Forces community and he knew that Dave worked for the government, traveled overseas frequently, and sometimes used a pseudo to help shield him from any repercussions of his work that might follow him back home.

Dave pulled into his drive to find a circus of fire trucks and police cars all flashing either red or blue lights depending on their affiliation. Fire hoses stretched across the drive and grass like fat snakes. Black smoke and white steam rose into the clear blue Virginia sky as carbon and water vapor advertised their transformation into gas. Many of the first responders' eyes turned toward Dave as he exited his truck.

Sheriff Dayton walked over to meet him. "Hey, Tom."

"Dave," the sheriff said, nodding. "It's bad. We found the housekeeper in the tub in the bathroom."

"Was she trying to get away from the flames?" Dave asked.

"No—no, she wasn't. Her head was wrapped in a bloody towel."

"What? That makes no sense."

"Dave, she was shot three times in the head."

At this, Dave went very still. "Are there any witnesses?" he asked.

"No, just the neighbor about a half-mile away who was coming home and saw the smoke. I have to ask: where were you an hour ago?"

"Not here. Come with me."

Dave and Tom walked around the house and behind the garage, entering it out of sight of the firefighters and other officers on the scene.

Power had been cut to the house, but the garage was on a UPS system so the battery back-up kept a few lights on. Dave walked over to the workbench and used a key from his truck keyring to unlock a panel in the wall. He swung the door open to reveal a very sophisticated video surveillance setup. Dave had cameras camouflaged around his property and throughout the house.

Folding down a portable keyboard, Dave tapped in some commands. A six-inch screen brightened and Dave started running the images backward until he saw a brown delivery van pull up to the house. Dave and Tom clearly saw the driver exit the delivery van with a package and go to the back door. The porch camera showed the back of the delivery man as he pushed his way into the house. They soon saw three other men get out of the van and post up beside the house.

Dave switched to a camera in the kitchen and watched in horror as the delivery man fired three rounds point-blank into his friend's forehead.

Dave looked at Tom. "Motherfucker," was all Tom could manage. "Do you know these guys?" he asked.

"No." Dave's face was set and grim.

"Are they foreign nationals?"

Dave looked at Tom for a long second, as if he was trying to decide if he could trust him. "No, I don't think so."

Dave inserted a disc into the drive and with a few more keystrokes, he had copied the camera files to the disc. He handed the evidence to Tom.

"I think you know more about this than you're telling me," Tom said, as they walked back to the house.

Dave didn't answer, nor look at Tom.

Finally, Dave asked, "Have you called Miranda's daughter?"

"No, we haven't gotten that far yet."

"Don't. She graduates from college tonight. I'll go by her house and tell her."

"Okay. Come by the office afterwards. Let's see if we can get some traction on this."

Dave nodded, but he had no intention of going to Tom's office. There would be "traction" on this all right, but Dave would be the one applying it.

Dave felt a little bad for the sheriff. Tom didn't know it, but the body count was about to go up.

83

CHAPTER 16

Retired Lt. General Mike Davis sat behind his desk across from Marcus Hanks, Hanks's flattop haircut matching the severity of his expression.

Mike Davis had commanded thirty thousand airmen as part of running a logistical command. He had manipulated contracts for overseas Base Exchanges—the Walmarts of the military—by shorting essential goods and selling them to local politicians, making both parties very wealthy.

Davis had used that money to fund a startup consulting firm, International Solutions, a cover for a mercenary training and contracting outfit. Now, he had his own private standing army made up of mostly retired special forces operators and foreign nationals. He polished their skills at his training center near Fredericksburg, Virginia and sold their services to the highest bidder.

General Davis sat patiently as Hanks, his Chief of Operations, debriefed his latest mission. Davis's mind raced, but his face showed no emotion. After Hanks finished, his boss asked, "Did you have to kill her?"

"Yes sir, we did. We weren't expecting her to be there, but once we pulled in the driveway and saw her car, we had to adapt in real time. There was no way to peel her out of the equation without her talking."

"And you didn't find the USB drive?"

"No, sir. If it was in the house, then it burned with everything else."

"Were you seen?"

"No, sir. No neighbors. We secured our search once our viz-ob spotted a car on the parallel road. That's when I contacted you. We were in and out clean."

"Okay, get a team together. Elevate our security posture to condition orange and post members at our headquarters building and at my home. I want a security bubble around me and this operation 24/7. He'll be coming for us, so don't take any chances. I also want you to put together a strike team. Find Walsh. I want him out of this, understand?"

"Yes sir, General Davis."

CHAPTER 17

Dave called Jax.

"They just torched my house."

"How bad is it?"

"Nothing I can't build back. They killed Miranda."

"What?"

"They must have gone there to search for the drive and she was there cleaning."

"Shit, I'm sorry man," Jax offered, and he truly meant it. He had met Miranda, and he knew she was especially protective of Dave after his family died. He also knew that Dave was helping support her and her daughter.

"I'm going to need some backup. Can I get Scott?" Dave asked.

"Yes, and I've got some good news. The girl escaped. Scotty's on the way to get her now. Meet us back at the Dungeon."

"I'll be there in two hours," Dave said, as he put his truck on cruise control and his mind into overdrive.

CHAPTER 18

A black Ford F-150 pulled in the parking lot of the Starbucks.

Lydia had been watching the parking lot for anyone or anything that looked remotely like the assholes who had grabbed her. The guy stepping out of the truck could be one of them.

He was buff with close cut blond hair. Dark Gatorz covered his eyes as he scanned the parking lot with a slow sweep of his head. He moved like a panther, smooth and graceful.

Pulling open the café door, his gaze casually swept the room as he walked to the counter to order. Lydia heard him ask for a grande white chocolate mocha with whip and two Sweet'N Low. That sure didn't sound like a tough-guy drink.

He got his coffee and slowly ambled over to the table next to Lydia's.

She stood up so that if needed, she could quickly exit the side door and run to the wooded lot behind the store. Noticing this, as he sat down he said in a low voice, "The Wizard sends his regards."

Lydia sat back down, still looking around the room to see if this was a trap. She played along and said, "Do you know Wiz?"

"Yes, I do."

"Would you mind taking me to him? My car was stolen, and I need a ride," she asked.

"Sure, let's go," said the man.

Her new BFF was trying to piece all this together when Lydia stood up, leaned over, and kissed him on the cheek. "Thank you so much for the use of your computer and phone," she said.

"You're welcome," he said to her back, as she walked out of the coffee shop with the blond guy.

Once out of earshot of the guy in the café he said, "I'm Scott. Jax sent me to get you. Are you okay?"

"Yes, I think so."

"Did they hurt you?"

"No. They locked me in a room, but I had the guard take me to the bathroom. The woman had a Taser."

"A Taser?"

"Yeah. She told me it would shock me, so I pulled the shower curtain down, wrapped it around the upper part of my body, and rushed her."

"Holy crap! That's genius! Did she shoot?"

"Yes, but the wires stuck in the plastic. I hit her with the lid from the toilet tank. You know, the heavy ceramic part."

"Holy shit! Remind me not to get on your bad side," Scotty said, laughing. This girl had as much guts and brains as any of the macho men he'd fought with. "How did you get out?"

"Well, she went down pretty hard and was out, but still breathing. I took her keys. There was no one else in the house so I unlocked the front door and made a run for it. We were in some neighborhood. I ran toward the freeway and found this Starbucks, then I borrowed the guy's computer I was sitting with. I found Jax's phone number and used his phone to call him."

"How did you find Jax's phone number?" Scotty knew that Jax was only listed in some highly classified databases not available to public browsers.

"I remembered his name and hacked into the power company's database," she said, as if she had simply Googled him.

Scotty slowly turned his head to look at this aberration sitting beside him. He had never met anyone quite like her.

CHAPTER 19

Dave had the cruise control set for seventy-three mph. His mind raced as he attempted to process all the information he had assimilated so far.

He needed to piece together the bigger picture and anticipate their next move.

Traitors seemed to have the same four motivators and he was sure he understood theirs. The acronym MICE covered them all: Money, Ideology, Coercion, Ego. He was also pretty sure that money and ego explained the motives for the co-conspirators listed on the USB drive.

Dave's subconscious registered the lack of traffic and the lone car on the side of the road. He noticed that the trunk was open, but saw no one standing around it. Dave began to apply the brakes, lightly at first, and as his training kicked in, more aggressively. He was now standing on the brakes, and his truck was bucking as the anti-skid brake function prevented the tires from sliding, allowing some measure of control while providing maximum stopping power.

His situational awareness saved his life. Two shooters emerged from the trees, firing full-auto M4 rifles. The two men were moving to the car to use as cover as they fired at Dave's truck. Dave pointed his three-thousand-pound truck directly at the car and stomped the gas.

The predators were now the prey.

They recognized, too late, that Dave was not going to stop. He was going to drive through the ambush. His path took him straight through the left rear quarter panel of the car at about thirty miles an hour with the kinetic energy from his truck transferring through the parked car and directly into the two men standing behind it, perfectly demonstrating Newton's Second Law of Motion. The ambushers flew into the air like puppets, landing twenty yards away at the edge of the tree line, lifeless.

Newton was no respecter of persons and the action-reaction side of his impact equation blew Dave's airbag into his face, knocking him unconscious.

CHAPTER 20

The water was icy cold, the surface a mirror. A thin layer of mist hovered above the water, giving the clear spring pond an eerie, but exciting feel.

Davy felt the early morning dew soak through his pants as he knelt on one knee and surveyed the area like a general surveying his battlefield prior to committing his leagues.

The smell of freshly cut hay and honeysuckle made an indelible imprint on his brain: smells that would always remind him of this place.

He noted where the trees slightly overhung the pool, offering his prey the opportunity of a meal as insects fell from the branches into the water.

He observed the occasional small, circular ripples as bass rose to the surface and inhaled a struggling bug. He looked for shade over the water where the trees blocked the sun and offered hiding places for bluegill and rock bass.

At sixteen, Davy was already a savvy fisherman.

Once his assessment was complete, he pieced together his fly rod, placed the reel on the handle, and strung the yellow line through the guides. He attached a leader to the line and tied his favorite deer hair Irresistible fly to the nearly invisible piece of thin, monofilament tippet tied to the end of the leader.

Easing up quietly to the edge of the pool, he stripped off some line and began to haul it into the air over his head in practiced strokes—bringing the rod up and stopping, allowing the line to extend behind him to flex the rod tip, then bringing his arm down, allowing the line to flow to the front for several repetitions.

With each cast, he could hear and feel the line shoot through the guides on his eight-weight fly rod. Eventually, he judged that he had fed enough line to reach his target area: the shade under the large weeping willow tree leaning over the water.

His line floated out in front of him and just kissed the surface of the water with almost no splash, his tiny lure imitating an unfortunate insect falling from one of the willow branches.

As soon as his fly landed, the water exploded. A huge, largemouth bass rose to the fly, striking from beneath and breaking the surface as he inhaled his easy meal.

The line immediately tightened, bowing his rod almost double. Davy felt the hook set. He pressed his finger against the bottom of the rod, trapping the line to keep tension on it. He released the pressure on the line slowly, allowing the big fish to run as the strong bass headed for deep water.

Davy loved the sound of his reel clicking against the drag that he had set just under the breaking point of the leader. The next few minutes were all about finesse.

Keeping the line tight enough to maintain a bend in the end of his fly-rod kept a constant load on the fish, thereby tiring it.

If he tried to horse the fish, it would break his light-weight line; if he allowed his line to go slack, there was a good chance the big bass would be able to spit out the hook.

After five minutes of sensing the strength of his quarry, anticipating his runs, and allowing just enough line out but never too much, he felt the fish begin to tire. He slowly retrieved some of his line with little resistance. The bass made fewer, more feeble attempts to flee.

Davy slowly reeled the now exhausted fish to the edge of the water. He reached down and scooped his landing net under it, bringing it to the surface. It was an eighteen-inch monster with a black stripe running down the middle of its olive-green flanks.

Davy used his forceps and grabbed the tiny gold hook by the shank, and then threaded it gently out of the corner of the fish's mouth.

He lowered the net and fish back into the water and wrapped his hand around the fish just in front of its tail. He pulled the net away and made a slow sideways waving motion with the bass to force water through his oxygen depleted gills. The huge fish snapped back to his fighting self, lunged away from his hand, and then headed for deeper water. Davy smiled as his conquest swam strongly away.

He turned to step away from the edge of the pond when suddenly he felt himself falling backward into the water. The shock of the cold water took his breath away. His clothes seemed to weigh him down, and he went under. He struggled to get to the surface. Davy was an excellent swimmer, but suddenly, he was completely uncoordinated; it was as if he could not remember how to swim. His arms and legs flailed.

"Davy! Davy!" he heard his mom call, but that was odd. He was over three miles from home. There was no way he could hear her.

Something floated over his face, and he couldn't breathe. He began struggling to pull it off.

"Dave!" he heard again as a hand grabbed his shoulder.

CHAPTER 21

Bright lights nearly blinded him.

Dave realized he had been dreaming of one of his favorite teenage memories: fly fishing in the backcountry near his home. He hadn't fished there in years, but he closed his eyes and could still see the ripples on the surface of the water as the huge bass rose to his fly.

Someone was saying, "Don't fight it. You need the oxygen mask on."

Dave squinted against the white room and fluorescent lights as a hand held his shoulder.

"Dave, it's Tom," he heard his friend, the sheriff, quietly whisper to him. "You're okay. You were in a car wreck. I was about five minutes behind you when I came upon the wreck."

Dave tried to turn his head toward the voice, but he was in a neck restraint.

"Don't try to move. They're still checking you out. You've been unconscious for about an hour," Tom told him.

Dave now remembered the ambush.

"Was anyone else at the scene?" he asked.

"Yeah, there were two guys in tactical gear, DOA. Neither one had ID on them. Both of them looked like they were former military. Your truck is at my impound lot with about thirty holes in it. The front end is pretty well crushed. It may be totaled. Also, two M4 rifles, with no serial numbers or manufacturer stamps, were found near the shooters. They looked like 'eighty percent' lowers someone built so they could not be traced. As soon as the doc clears you, we're going to have a talk. There have been three violent deaths in my county in one day. We don't get three deaths like this in a year, and you seem to be the constant in all three."

CHAPTER 22

FOUR MONTHS EARLIER

Tarik Basik's cell phone buzzed in his pocket. He was enjoying a strong tea at the Tee Haus across the street from his office on the Operngasse in Donau City. His caller ID showed his sister was calling.

She was an au pair for a family of four in the small town of Linz. He recalled her telling him that the two children were well-behaved and the parents were kind to her. The father was a German history professor at the university; the mother was a lawyer.

"Hello, Amina!"

"Tarik, how are you?"

"I'm well, and you?"

"Very good. The children are little angels. They mind well, as only little Austrians can," she said seriously.

Amina was always serious. Tarik could not remember the last time he'd heard his sister laugh.

Her laughter had died along with their parents, two smaller brothers, and seventy-three innocent civilians on April 15, 1999—the day a United States F-16 fighter aircraft bombed a refugee convoy in Kosovo.

Tarik and Amina were traveling with their family and several hundred refugees on the road between Prizren and Djakovica on that horrific day. They were asleep in the bed of the truck with what little furnishings their family had left. The bomb fragments sliced through the cab of the truck, cutting his father, mother, and brothers, Amar and Daris, to shreds.

Tarik and Amina lay on the side of the road as the jet roared away, their ears ringing from the explosions. They were seeing, but not believing, the carnage before them.

The horror washed over them like a tidal wave. Bodies and parts of bodies were scattered across the road and the fields. Vehicles were burning, and black smoke stung their eyes and noses. The smell of cooked flesh would forever be imprinted on their olfactory nerves. Tarik pulled his sister to him and held her head to his shoulder, trying to prevent her from seeing what had already been etched in her brain.

Sitting in the Tee Haus, Tarik realized that he had closed his eyes as he recalled the horror of that day. As always, the memory rode just below the surface, as real as the day it happened.

He opened his eyes and looked at the Danube River through the window of the tea shop, and breathed deeply, trying to relax. The horror was still there, but tamped down and held in place by hatred for the ones who had killed his family.

He had dedicated his life to avenging them, but Tarik was not the type to strap on a suicide vest or shoot a few American tourists with an AK-47. He wanted every American infidel to feel the depth of pain and sorrow he felt. He wanted to terrorize them, to make them live in fear. Tarik also understood that grand plans required grand amounts of money.

****

Tarik had to hold down many jobs, most on the fringe of legality, to work his way through high secondary school in Belgrade.

He moved to Vienna as soon as he had saved enough money to attend university there. He studied banking and secured a position at the Austrian Bank as an investment broker.

Tarik built a reputation as an intuitive broker. His sharp analytical skills allowed him to increase the fortunes of some of Austria's wealthiest citizens. Along the way, he developed relationships with several rich Arab businessmen, helping them to compound their wealth while providing the additional services of hiding and laundering their money—for a fee, of course.

He also secretly ascribed to the radicalized Salafi Jihadist movement. The fundamentalist Salafis believe in a return to the original ways of Islam. Only his sister and two of his closest allies knew of his role with the Salafis. He had used his two allies as cut-outs to fund small terrorist activities around the world, always striking at American interests in unique and unpredictable ways.

Tarik was the shadow architect of the Boston Marathon bombing. He was funding and supplying the Syrian Jihad effort, in part, to get the US looking in a direction other than their homeland. He'd been planning a major attack on US soil for some time, but he had been unable to obtain the necessary nuclear or biological components.

****

"Tarik. Tarik! Are you there?"

He realized his thoughts had wandered again. Amina was shouting his name over the phone.

"Yes, sister—I'm here."

"It scares me sometimes when you drift off like that. I have some very interesting news . . . can you meet me for dinner tonight? Dr. Dorner and his wife are taking the kids to the cinema, and I need to see you."

She paused for a second then added, "It is important."

"Okay, I will meet you tonight at the café on Tummelplatz in Linz at eight o'clock."

"Yes, I will be there! I will see you tonight! I love you, brother!"

"I love you too, sister."

Tarik disconnected as he walked back to the bank, oblivious of the beautiful Austrian spring weather.

CHAPTER 23

Lost in thought, Tarik barely registered the two-hour drive to the Café Schloss to meet Amina.

Lately, he had become increasingly consumed with executing a plan to destroy the devils in America. He felt a clock counting down in his head and soul; an idea was forming. He had the will and the financial resources, but not the weapon of mass destruction needed to fulfill his plan. However, Tarik had contacts in the US government who he could very skillfully manipulate to his will.

Years ago, when one of his Muslim clients had asked Tarik to find investors interested in buying mineral rights in Iraq and Afghanistan, he had inserted himself into a plan to sell rights to several high-ranking US military officers. Of note, Tarik had been doing business with American General Mike Davis. He'd been referred to General Davis as a source to launder the tremendous amount of cash generated by selling stolen American goods diverted from foreign Base Exchanges.

The mineral rights plan Tarik proposed to General Davis showed potential for staggering profits by selling oil from Iraq, and rare earth elements from Afghanistan, which were essential for the production of most modern military equipment. As Tarik hoped, General Davis pulled other influential men into the scheme.

In the early years, Tarik transferred large amounts of his personal money to Davis's account, posing as buyers of the mineral rights. Once Davis and his cronies trusted him, Tarik simply cooked the books to make it appear that the investors were amassing a fortune. The more dollars the investors sent, the more Tarik falsely inflated their bottom line.

Tarik had helped General Davis and his fellow investors build a fortune valued at over five hundred million dollars—at least on paper. Tarik chuckled at the thought of the American idiots actually trying to resell mineral rights in Afghanistan and Iraq.

Davis found a few other greedy investors and managed to sell about 120 million dollars of mineral rights, promptly depositing that money in Tarik's bank account to hide it from the IRS. Tarik used the American's money to finance terrorist activities against America; the irony was sweet.

Tarik eventually learned that Davis's partners were Warren Battles of the DNI, Secretary of Defense Allen Greensmith, and Foster Hillum, a major defense contractor. Tarik held those contacts as the most precious investment he owned. Having direct access to the central nervous system of the US government was better than a vault full of gold bullion. He didn't know when he would need to cash in on that investment, but he knew it would pay huge dividends.

As he arrived, he saw Amina's brown Hyundai in the parking lot. Amina was sitting at a table toward the back of the café, somewhat isolated from the rest of the diners. She waved as he came in. He hugged her, giving her the traditional Kosovar cheek kisses.

"I've already ordered tea for us. You look tired, Tarik. Are you working too hard?"

"No, I'm okay. I just have a lot on my mind."

"I've also ordered a maze platter."

"Good, I'm hungry."

The waiter arrived with a white china tea service and the maze platter containing an array of small plates with cheeses, cucumbers, melons, assorted stuffed vegetables, and hot pepper sauce. They prepared their tea before speaking again. Amina looked around to be sure no one was within earshot.

She leaned in and whispered, "I overheard something you might find important."

Tarik looked her in the eyes and knew this was not gossip, but information to further the cause.

"Dr. Dorner was late for dinner two evenings ago, and I overheard him telling his wife, Anna, that he had been contacted by a reporter. The reporter learned of a secret bunker near Linz while researching old US intelligence reports dating back to World War II. He said the Nazis built a very large underground research facility to conduct nuclear and biological testing. The doctor told her that the government wanted him to go to the bunker as a historian and help verify it was actually from the Nazi era. He said he spent almost all day underground, as it was a very large complex. It had not been opened for over seventy years. Dr. Dorner then whispered to her, but I heard anyway.

"He told her there was no nuclear material in that bunker, but there was a very large supply of Sarin poison in well-preserved containers. This seemed to frighten his wife, as Anna asked if they should move away for a while.

He told her no, not yet at least, but they may want to go on holiday if they decided to move the canisters. The doctor said the Sarin was so deadly that if they made a mistake in handling it, it would kill thousands."

Tarik was cautiously elated. This could be the answer to his prayers, delivered to him after being hidden from the world for over seven decades.

He would need to move fast before the news was widespread. Tarik lost his appetite. He was already making plans to get possession of one of the world's most deadly poisons.

Tarik smiled through the rest of the meal, talking little, but thinking at the speed of light.

"Sister, you have been diligent to pay attention and to bring this information to me. Do you know if the doctor has made any notes about the bunker?"

"I have not seen any, but he always keeps his laptop with him and he may have written information on it."

"Can you check to see?"

"Yes, I will try, but he keeps it very close to him."

"Okay, we must move with haste before the world descends on this small town."

"I will call you tomorrow."

"You are brave, sister. I love you."

"I love you too, brother."

"I must go and make some preparations."

"Please be careful."

Tarik hugged his sister and walked to his car, mentally planning the destruction of the United States of America.

CHAPTER 24

Three days later, Amina awoke with a sense of unease.

Dr. Dorner and his wife had been very good to her. They paid her well and treated her kindly. The children, Felix and Emma, were pleasant and respectful as well as intelligent and always eager to learn new things. Amina loved teaching the children about her regional culture and showing them how she cooked traditional meals of Burek, and the apple dessert, Tufahija.

What she was about to do would betray the doctor and his family. She knew the cause was more important than her relationship with her adopted Austrian family; yet, she felt pangs of guilt at the thought of breaking their trust.

Amina needed to get to the room Dr. Dorner used as his home office before he awoke.

The house was silent as she slipped quietly into the room; his laptop was on top of the cluttered desk.

She clutched the red thumb drive Tarik had sent by courier yesterday. He'd sent a red one and a black one and had been very careful to explain that she needed to insert the red thumb drive in the computer before she powered it up, as it would defeat the doctor's password.

She opened the laptop, inserted the red thumb drive, and pressed the power button. The computer began to hum and the security screen lit up, asking for the password. Tarik had instructed her to press the "Enter" button, and she did. The security screen went away instantly, as he said it would.

She now needed to insert the black thumb drive into another USB port, and it would automatically download the entire contents of the computer. As soon as the thumb drive was inserted, a dialog box on the screen popped up and asked, "Begin Download?" She had been instructed to hit "Y" for yes, and she did. The computer began clicking again and small pictures of file folders started flying toward the thumb drive icon.

"Amina, what are you doing?"

Amina jumped, startled by the doctor standing in the doorway, looking a little confused, but also wary.

"I was just, uh . . . just looking," she stammered.

The doctor walked over and looked at the screen. He understood immediately what she was doing, just not why.

"Why?" he asked.

Before she could reply, the front door of the house exploded as it was blown from its hinges by two shotgun blasts.

While Amina was still trying to understand what was happening, a man carrying an AK-47 and wearing a black shemagh along with a pouch for rifle magazines entered the doctor's office. He raised his rifle and fired point-blank into the doctor's head, sending blood and brains splashing against the ceiling and back wall.

The attacker walked to the desk, picked up the laptop, and placed it in a canvas satchel hanging over his shoulder. He said to Amina in Albanian: "Let's go."

Amina heard three distinct but muted gunshots come from the bedrooms. Another man, dressed like the first, came down the stairs with a shotgun slung across his chest. He also carried a pistol with a long silencer in his right hand.

She noticed two five-liter cans of gasoline placed by the front door. One man grabbed a can and went upstairs. The other man poured gasoline on the doctor's body, splashing the rest around the office and across the furniture and floors.

When he'd finished, he ushered Amina out the front door and into a white van. Still not wanting to believe what was happening, she asked, "The children?" The man just looked at her with dead eyes.

The other man exited the house and paused as he cleared the front porch. He pulled a road flare from his vest, ignited it, and tossed it into the house. There was a loud *whoosh* as the house was engulfed in flames. The fire spread quickly, breaking windows and feeding itself with oxygen.

Amina could smell the smoke as she sat in the back of the van.

She covered her mouth with her hand as she saw the flames bursting through the roof. She felt exactly as she had on that horrific day standing in the field, seeing her family destroyed by the actions of a murderous bomber.

CHAPTER 25

Amina sobbed quietly during the entire two-hour trip. The two men unwrapped their heads and stored their vests and guns in a compartment hidden in the floor of the van. They rode in silence, carefully obeying the traffic laws and blending in with the dozens of delivery vans on the A1 route to Vienna.

On the outskirts of town, they turned north toward the 19th district of Doubling.

They pulled into the circular drive of a magnificent mansion with colonial columns and beautifully manicured lawns. They opened the side door and had to help Amina out of the van. She was in a daze; her world had just been turned upside down.

The two men carefully led her up the steps and through the front door. They escorted her to a sitting room that had elaborate chandeliers and white overstuffed sofas. The parquet wood floors were shined to a mirror finish and perfectly appointed with expensive woven rugs in both silk and wool.

Tarik came into the room and hugged her. He sat her on one of the sofas.

"Why?" she asked.

"It had to be. We could not leave any trace."

"The children?" she pleaded.

Tarik offered no comment.

"Now we will search his computer and see if the doctor has written about the bunker."

"How did you know I would fail?"

"I didn't, but I had to plan for that. One of the thumb drives had a listening device implanted. We heard him question you. We were prepared to act, and we did. You did not fail. It is how it works sometimes."

Amina looked around, suddenly aware of her surroundings.

"Whose house is this?" she asked.

"Mine. I lease it out to wealthy travelers, but sometimes I use it for meetings."

"I need to lie down. I feel sick."

Tarik tilted his head to one of his men who helped Amina up the stairs to a spacious bedroom. He quietly closed the door as she collapsed on the large platform bed.

Ahmed handed the doctor's laptop to Tarik. Tarik opened the computer that still had the red thumb drive inserted into the USB port. He began scrolling through the doctor's files.

He found one labeled "*Underground Nazi Weapons Factory.*"

He opened the file and read that the underground, seventy-five-acre site had been secretly built by the Nazis at the beginning of World War II using slave labor. The report went on to describe the killing of the 40,000 prisoners who built the bunkers in order to protect the Nazi's secret lab.

The next file was the one he was hoping to find. It contained an inventory of the bunker contents discovered to date.

CHAPTER 26

Tarik printed off the construction plans for the bunker from Dr. Dorner's computer.

The good doctor had marked the location of the Sarin and described the containers that held the deadly poison. There were fifty-two of them. They were approximately one meter tall and dark gray, with yellow stripes around each cylinder. The doctor had even taken pictures of the cylinders.

Dr. Dorner's notes revealed the investigators were in the process of permanently sealing the room containing the cylinders.

Tarik had to get there before that process could happen.

He asked Ahmed and Hamza, the two men who had captured the computer, if they knew any warriors in Linz. In order to give him time to develop a plan for the use of the deadly gas, he would need to remove the cylinders from the bunker surreptitiously to avoid an all-out panic and a worldwide search for the missing Sarin. He needed time without the hounds on his trail.

Neither Ahmed nor Hamza knew of any Jihadists in Linz.

"We will have to do it ourselves," said Tarik.

"Ahmed, take Hamza and go to Linz. Find out who the labor crews are that will be sealing the bunker. Do whatever it takes to get on that crew. We will begin making a plan to steal some of the cylinders and will execute it as soon as you let me know you are on the crew. I'll start putting together a transportation and storage plan for the cylinders. Hurry . . . Allah has only given us a few days to begin our Jihad against the most terrible Satan." Staring each man in the eyes, he said, "You will not fail."

Both nodded in agreement.

CHAPTER 27

Ahmed and Hamza traveled back to Linz the next day in a nondescript car. They rented a single room for a week in a run-down hotel on the edge of town.

A few discreet inquiries at the local mosque revealed the names of some of the laborers who would be pouring the concrete to seal the bunker rooms. The night before the work was to begin, they paid a visit to two brothers who had been assigned to the job. They lived in a high-density apartment building occupied mostly by third country nationals, many of them laboring at menial jobs to send money back to their families in other parts of the world.

Ahmed knocked on the flimsy wooden door.

Adn, the older of the two brothers, cautiously opened the door a crack. *Who could possibly be at their door?* They knew very few people. They only worked, ate meager rations at home, and slept to work the next day.

"As-salamu alaikum," Ahmed offered. *Peace be upon you.*

"Wa-Alaikum-Salaam," *And upon you Peace*, the brother Adn returned, though still wary.

"The imam said you would know where we can find work."

Adn opened the door fully.

"Please come in."

"This is my brother, Hamza," Ahmed said, as they entered the apartment.

Adn noticed the two men looking over the one-room apartment.

While Ahmed was actually conducting a quick security scan, Adn thought he was appraising his tiny apartment. It was sparsely furnished with a broken-down couch, a small card table, two chairs, a recliner, and a two-burner heating plate.

"We live very humbly here," Adn explained. "We send almost all of our money back to our families. Work is very difficult to come by. We recently got jobs digging in a bunker near here. It is very dangerous work, but the pay is good."

"Is there work there for my brother and I?" asked Ahmed.

"I am not sure. I will ask tomorrow."

"That would be good. My brother and I have no family to send money to. They were killed in the war. We would be willing to pay you part of our wages to work, and even some rent to sleep on your floor here. We have a car."

"You have a car?" Adn asked, surprised.

"Yes, a very old one, but it runs and we have all the papers—well, maybe not all of the papers are official," Ahmed said, smiling.

"Ahhhh," Adn said, nodding his head at his new friend's shared conspiracy.

"Then we could ride to work with our two rich friends and avoid bus fare."

"Exactly," replied Ahmed.

"Do you have a place to stay tonight?" Adn asked.

"No," lied Ahmed.

"Then you stay here tonight; no charge." Adn smiled at his potential source of future revenue.

"We will need to get our things from our car."

"Okay, I will get some blankets for you. One of you can sleep on the couch and the other on the reclining chair."

Ahmed and Hamza did not speak until they were down the steps and outside near the car.

"Do we kill them tonight?" Hamza asked, speaking for the first time since they arrived at the apartment.

"No. Let us see if we can get on the job legitimately first. It will leave fewer questions and give us more time to execute our friend's plan."

"This place is a sty for pigs," Hamza observed.

"Yes, brother, it is, but not as bad as Afghanistan or Syria, yes? And no one is trying to drop a bomb on your sorry head!" Ahmed laughed.

"No, not that bad," replied Hamza, solemnly. He never laughed.

Ahmed reached under the front seat of the car and retrieved a small cell phone hidden in the springs of the seat cushion.

He dialed the one number that he was permitted to dial from that phone. As soon as the connection was made, he pushed the "star" and the "pound" buttons and heard a series of tones. His connection was now secure.

"We have an in," he said.

"How long?" was the reply.

"I will know tomorrow how aggressive we need to be."

"Time is short."

"I know. I will have more details about getting hired tomorrow when our hosts return from work."

"I have had some special equipment built. I want to meet with you tomorrow at 1100 hours. We will need to be ready to execute our plan two days from now."

"We should be ready by then, Insha'Allah." *God willing.*

"Yes, Insha'Allah."

Ahmed disconnected, turned off the phone, and replaced it under the seat.

He shivered from the chill of the night as he locked the door of his car.

He opened the trunk and retrieved their small, worn backpacks containing an extra shirt and underwear.

Hidden in the very bottom of each pack was a black canvas bag that contained a Walther P22 pistol and an LCW Predator silencer.

"Let us go. We need our rest. We have much to do in the next few days," he said as he handed Hamza a backpack.

Hamza nodded, following his brother and leader up the stairs with the same devotion he had always felt as they travelled through Jihadist hell and back.

CHAPTER 28

The next morning, Ahmed checked his phone at exactly 0900 and found a text from Tarik.

Meet at Sudpark Linz at 1100.

Ahmed knew that was the industrial park by the Danube River. There was no need to reply. Tarik expected him to be there.

They arrived at exactly 1100 hours.

Tarik was already there in the white van they had recently used, and it blended in perfectly with all the other delivery vans in the industrial park.

Ahmed nodded to Hamza, who exited the car and moved a short distance away from the meeting to provide overwatch security. Six steps from the car, Hamza turned and lifted a small handheld radio up and keyed the microphone. Ahmed heard the squelch crackle on his handheld radio and pressed his own transmit button breaking the squelch on Hamza's radio. Hamza nodded; their radio checks completed, he trotted off to take up his sentry duties.

Ahmed got out of his car and climbed into the passenger's seat of the white van.

Tarik began the briefing without greeting. "We determined we need three of the cylinders containing the

Sarin poison gas." He reached back and lifted the corner of a tarp for Ahmed to see three perfect replicas of the Sarin gas cylinders and three slightly larger green tanks. "The green tanks have a false bottom, so we can put the fake cylinders inside them to get them into the bunker, and hide the real cylinders as we bring them out. Our ambulance crew will wheel the green tanks into the bunker where they will remove the fake cylinders and place three of the Sarin cylinders inside them to take back to the ambulance. The fake cylinders are necessary to leave behind so as to disguise the fact that three of the Sarin cylinders are missing. Your job is to create a diversion to get everyone out of the bunker. You will then use explosives to seal that area of the bunker to delay discovery that three Sarin cylinders are missing."

Ahmed nodded. "I can do that. I will need some supplies."

"Tell me what you need, but we must act quickly. If the national authorities discover the type of gas that is in that bunker, they will send many men to protect it. I will be ready to act tomorrow. I have the ambulance crew standing by."

"I will have the list ready for you tonight."

With that, Ahmed exited the van and looked around for Hamza. He was standing by a loading dock with a view of the entire parking lot. Ahmed reached in his pocket and keyed the transmit button on his radio twice, breaking squelch on Hamza's radio and signaling him to return to the car.

"We have much work to do, my brother," Ahmed said, as they drove out of the parking lot and back to the apartment. Ahmed spent the rest of the afternoon explaining the plan to Hamza. Hamza nodded at the appropriate times, neither adding to, nor questioning any of the details.

CHAPTER 29

Ahmed sent a secure text to Tarik with the equipment he would need. It wasn't much.

As a Jihadist, he had learned to improvise using whatever was available—usually the enemy's own resources and assumptions against them.

Exactly four hours later, a red Ford Focus pulled up in front of the apartment building where Ahmed and Hamza had spent the previous night. The driver never made eye contact with the man who approached the car from the rear, or with the man who stayed near the front fender with his hand inside his jacket.

The driver opened the trunk using an interior lever. As soon as the man at the rear of the car slammed the trunk closed, the driver hit the gas and sped away.

Ahmed lugged the heavy black duffel bag up the stairs and into the Adn's apartment. The first items he removed were two heavy, stiff black hoods made from old Kevlar bulletproof vests. They had long industrial-strength zip ties around the bottom for quickly cinching them closed. There was a four-inch circular patch of white material stitched on the side of each hood. The white circle was sewn to indicate where a four-inch hole had been cut in the Kevlar.

He placed the hoods aside and removed two tear gas grenades, four flash-bang grenades, and four white smoke grenades. They would need all of those for distraction purposes.

Ahmed then removed two gas masks that would protect them from the tear gas in the bunker and six blocks of Semtex explosive wrapped with Det-Cord. The pull-ring initiators had variable delay settings.

He also removed a small camera, a tiny printer, and a small laminating machine.

Also included was a box of white cotton cleaning cloths and a spray bottle of Armor All, stored in a Ziploc bag. Another Ziploc bag contained several rolled up twelve-inch-long zip ties. Lining the bottom of the bag were two folded black body bags.

Ahmed placed the bag of zip ties in his back pocket and all the rest of the items back in the bag in the same order they were packed originally. He then placed the bag out of sight between the couch and the wall.

Hamza went to the small kitchen and set a pot of water on one of the burner plates and began boiling water to make tea. They had about two hours before the brothers returned from work.

CHAPTER 30

Ahmed sat on the right end of the couch with his Walther P22 pistol—suppressor attached— tucked between the cushion and the arm where he could pull it out easily. Hamza moved one of the kitchen chairs closer to the back side of the entry door to allow him to simply stand up and block any retreat, should the brothers attempt it.

Adn and his brother were not Jihadists. They had never fought for their lives. He doubted they would understand what was happening until it was too late.

They heard the key in the door and the brothers entered and closed the door behind them.

"Hello, my brothers," Ahmed greeted.

"Hello, friends," Adn replied.

"How was the work today?"

"It was good. We spent most of the day getting ID cards, training on gas masks, and reviewing evacuation plans for the bunker."

Adn reached inside his shirt and retrieved his photo ID card attached to a chain around his neck and showed it to Ahmed.

"I inquired about work for you and your brother. They say they may have more work next week after they get the bunker mapped out completely. You are welcome to stay here until that time."

"Yes, brother, I think I *will* stay here for a while."

The tone of Ahmed's remark sounded a bit off to Adn; he looked from Ahmed to Hamza and back.

Ahmed stood up, drawing his pistol, and pointed it at Adn's head.

Hamza drew his pistol as well and pointed it at Adn's brother's head.

"Sit in the chair," Ahmed ordered Adn.

"What is this? We have nothing to steal! We gave you shelter. You are our religious brothers!" Adn protested.

"Yes, brother, you are correct. Now sit in that chair," Ahmed demanded.

Adn's brother also sat as Hamza pressed the barrel of his gun against his head.

Hamza used the white plastic zip ties to bind the brothers' hands to the chairs where they sat while Ahmed kept his pistol pointed at them.

Ahmed removed the ID cards from each brother's neck.

"Tell me about the security at the bunker. We heard there may be gold stored there, and we want to take it. If you cooperate, we will leave you tied up and be gone tomorrow," Ahmed said, to give them hope.

"There is very little security yet. They said it will take a week for them to get the national government involved. They said the first thing they will do is take an inventory. We are to help them do that. But they have not mentioned anything about gold, only some munitions from the war. We saw many gray metal cylinders with yellow stripes. No one has mentioned gold."

"Very good. Of course, they would not tell you. They want to keep the gold for themselves."

"Brother, there is no gold," Adn pleaded. "I walked through the whole bunker today."

Ahmed retrieved the two black hoods and handed one to Hamza.

He nodded his head, and they moved behind the seated brothers and quickly put the hoods over their heads. Their shouts were muted through the heavy material.

Ahmed and Hamza pulled the zip tie attached to the bottom of the hoods tight against the brother's necks as they screamed and rocked in their chairs.

Ahmed and Hamza placed the muzzle of their suppressors in the center of the white patches of cloth and pulled the triggers.

Two quiet pops, sounding like a soft clap of the hands, and the brothers were sent to their reward.

Their heads dropped forward. The Kevlar material contained the .22 caliber bullets inside the hoods as they exited their foreheads. The heavy zip ties constricting their necks contained the blood and brain matter inside the sealed hoods.

They removed the two body bags and opened them in front of the chairs where the dead men sat, still tied at the hands. They cut the zip ties on their wrists and allowed each body to pitch forward into their black vinyl coffin. They zipped the bags closed and stacked them behind the couch against the wall like cordwood.

Ahmed took the two IDs to the kitchen and looked them over carefully. There were no holograms embossed into the laminate. That was good.

He tacked a bed sheet to the wall of the kitchen for a backdrop and pulled one of the death chairs in front of it. He had Hamza sit in the chair.

He studied the size of the photo and moved just the right distance away and took a photo of Hamza. He had to repeat the process three times to get the photo orientation to match as closely as possible to the dead brothers' IDs.

He had Hamza duplicate the process and take his picture.

Once satisfied with the photos, Ahmed connected the small color printer to the camera and printed them on glossy cardstock. He plugged in the laminating machine. While waiting for it to warm up, he trimmed the photos to the proper size.

Ahmed carefully placed his picture over Adn's photo, sandwiched it in between two pieces of clear plastic, and fed it through the laminating machine, repeating the process for Hamza's ID.

When finished he could see only a slight bulge where the two photos were stacked up. The IDs would pass a cursory check. It would take someone trained in ID card fraud to detect the difference. Ahmed was sure that level of expertise was not yet in place at the bunker.

They trimmed the hole in the new laminate, threaded the neck chains, and dropped the still warm cards in their pockets. Ahmed and Hamza spent the next thirty minutes using the white cotton cloths and the Armor All to wipe down anything they had touched over the past two days.

CHAPTER 31

Ahmed and Hamza arrived at the checkpoint early, but waited until many of the workers had lined up to enter. They needed to spend one day on the job to understand the security protocols and get the layout of the bunker.

They passed easily through the ID checkpoint. The guard barely glanced at their newly minted ID cards.

Following the crowd onto the bunker site, they passed through a large parking lot being utilized by the supervisors; Ahmed made careful note of the vehicles. He also observed that the guards were checking the ID cards of the occupants, but they weren't searching the incoming vehicles. They only searched the vehicles leaving the site.

That was perfect.

He noticed a Mercedes UNIMOG truck with a canvas-covered bed and decided that would be the truck he would use. He would follow that truck to where it parked for the night and hide his gear in it, allowing the unsuspecting driver to deliver the items he would need the next day.

Ahmed and Hamza spent the day wandering from room to room in the bunker, pretending to look for their assigned work location. The typical confusion of a new work site allowed them freedom of movement that would not be possible in just a few more days. Their recon for the day was worthwhile. They discovered the location of the yellow striped gas canisters, the entry and exit points, and where they needed to place their explosive charges to seal off the room with the canisters. Ahmed and Hamza also discovered a place to hide while the rest of the bunker was being evacuated.

That night, before returning to their dingy hotel room, they followed the UNIMOG truck to a lot where it would be parked for the night. The driver locked the truck and then left the area in his personal vehicle. Ahmed and Hamza easily defeated the truck's locks, storing the gear they would need behind the driver's fold-down seat. In the morning, they would follow the truck until they saw it safely on the site. They would then park offsite and take a bus with the rest of the laborers back to the front gate.

They intended to escape with their prize in the back of the ambulance, or die trying. As was usual for them, there was no middle ground.

Success or death were the only two options.

The next morning, the first part of the plan went flawlessly. They entered the bunker site without being challenged. They removed the black duffle bag containing the tear gas, explosives, and smoke grenades from the UNIMOG truck and hid it in the spot they had identified the previous day. They concealed their small, handheld radios in their pockets.

Once they were ready to execute their plan, they placed the explosives and timers in wheelbarrows, covering them with trash. They moved the wheelbarrows to the strategic locations selected the day before. Their objectives were to maximize the damage to the bunker and to seal off the room housing the gas as they were leaving.

At exactly 1000 hours, Ahmad and Hamza entered the gas room and placed gas masks over their faces. They pulled the pins on two of the tear gas grenades and dropped them on the concrete floor. Within seconds, men began yelling, "Gas! Gas! Gas! Get out! Get out!"

A stampede to the exits ensued; panic reined—a beautiful thing for Ahmed to watch.

Within minutes, an ambulance pulled up to the entrance. Had anyone thought about it, they would have realized it was impossible that a call could have been made and an emergency vehicle responded that quickly. Two men in dark blue uniforms jumped from the ambulance and yanked the back doors open. In the confusion, no one noticed them putting on gas masks and removing a large cart with three green oxygen tanks. The crush of panicked workers, eyes watering, noses running, many retching, provided a formidable challenge to the ambulance workers going against the flow.

Tear gas billowed from the entrances. Two white smoke grenades were added to the mixture, thickening and reducing the visibility even further. For added effect, Ahmed and Hamza threw a few flash-bang grenades near the entrance. The extremely loud bangs and bright flashes served to discourage any "heroes" from trying to re-enter the bunker.

Ahmed saw the two attendants appear through the smoke and gas, pushing the cart. The attendants followed him into the gas room. Unbuckling the three green oxygen tanks and laying them on their sides, they used a spanner to unscrew the bottom of the tanks and remove the smaller replica Sarin cylinders. They stood the replica cylinders beside the remaining authentic Sarin cylinders, carefully slid three of the real Sarin cylinders inside the fake oxygen tanks, and reattached the false bottoms. They then placed the oxygen tanks containing the Sarin cylinders on the cart and strapped them down, pushing them toward the entrance.

Ahmed and Hamza set the timers on the explosives and ran to catch up with the attendants as they pushed the cart outside and loaded it into the ambulance. The brothers climbed into the back as the driver roared away with lights and siren on, clearing a path through the crowd. They were less than half a mile from the front gate when the ground shook as the Semtex explosives detonated, sealing off the bunker as planned.

In the back of the ambulance, Ahmed and Hamza used special chemical wipes to neutralize and clear the strong tear gas from their eyes and mucus membranes. Feeling the explosions brought a small grin to Ahmed's face and a slight nod of the head from Hamza.

CHAPTER 32

"We have it," Ahmed relayed over the encrypted phone.

"Excellent. You know where to go. I will meet you there," said Tarik.

Three hours later, Ahmed, Hamza, and the two men who impersonated the ambulance attendants had changed their clothes and transferred their deadly cargo to another truck. They burned both the car and the ambulance at a remote construction site.

Arriving at a secure facility near Vienna, the driver looked directly into the security camera and the gate slid open. They drove around back and carefully unloaded the Sarin gas canisters onto the dock. Men in hazmat suits took the cart with the three green tanks, wheeling it into an environmentally sealed room. Seeing this, Ahmed shook his head; he and Hamza had handled the same tanks with their bare hands and ridden in the back of the ambulance with their feet resting on the tanks for over two hours.

Tarik, who seldom displayed emotion, hugged both Ahmed and Hamza.

"You have successfully completed a mighty mission, brothers. Allah smiles on you."

"Thank you, brother," replied Ahmed. "The plan worked well."

"Yes. News networks are reporting that a booby trap, apparently left by the Nazis, exploded in the bunker, collapsing a large portion of it. No mention of the poison gas was made. They will keep that part a secret from the public."

Tarik led the two men into a large laboratory with thick plate glass windows separating them from the environmental room. They could see men in self-contained hazmat gear working on the green oxygen tanks. Each tank was strapped to a stainless-steel table. They removed the bottom of the tanks and extracted the smaller cylinders of Sarin.

"They will test the poison gas to see if it is still viable. Sarin must be carefully stored to maintain its potency. These tanks are very old, so there is a chance that the gas is no longer poisonous," said Tarik.

Ahmed and Hamza watched as the technicians in the environmental room connected a hose to the valve on one of the Sarin cylinders. After placing the cylinder in a sealed cabinet, they connected the hose from it to an external valve. A technician opened a set of curtains covering the window of a small cubicle adjacent to the environmental room. Inside, an old man with a gray beard and greasy hair was strapped to a chair that was bolted to the floor. Leather straps secured his wrists and ankles. Electrical leads were attached to a heart monitor.

Once the preparations were complete, the technicians exited the cubicle, sealed the door, and looked at Tarik, who nodded his assent. The technician pulled a handle, opening the valve on the top of the cylinder and allowing a small amount of the poison to enter the cubicle. Immediately, flashing lights and warning horns signaled the presence of poisonous gas in the environmental cubicle.

Video cameras were focused on the old man's face. His nose began to run instantly; his pupils constricted as his eyes widened in fear. His chest began to heave as his muscles began to lose the ability to move his diaphragm. He began vomiting, defecating, and urinating uncontrollably. In less than a minute, he began to jerk violently and fell forward against his restraints. Within two minutes, he was comatose.

The heart monitor began emitting a tone that revealed the obvious.

Two minutes and thirty seconds had elapsed since releasing the gas.

The technicians looked at Tarik, fear evident behind the huge face masks of their hazmat suits. For his part, Tarik looked more determined than ever as the technicians closed the curtains on the old man.

"Now, we plan the next phase of our attack," Tarik voiced to no one in particular.

CHAPTER 33

Over the next two weeks, Tarik was completely absorbed in devising a plan to utilize the weapon of mass destruction he now possessed.

During that time, testing of the gas at the laboratory continued. To Tarik's satisfaction, all three of the cylinders had been very well preserved. The deadly Sarin remained as pristine and potent as the day it was hellishly conceived.

A plan to employ the poison was slowly evolving; he would need to get the Sarin into the US water supply. He needed to select one city, but would need several access points within that city.

US municipal water supplies are surrounded by high fences, many with security patrols. Simply driving up and dropping the poison into the water was not feasible.

He needed a method to disperse the Sarin into the water from the air, but using an airplane and a pilot was out of the question. "Crop duster" type aircraft were under close watch due to the many national alerts that those planes could be used to spread poison.

However, there might be another way.

Americans had a newfound obsession with small, remote-controlled craft. They called them Unmanned

Aerial Vehicles, or UAVs. Tarik believed he could put the poison in small UAVs, launch them over municipal water sources, and disperse the chemical into the water.

He met with Ahmed, Hamza, and two of his scientists to discuss the plan, ultimately deciding that Washington, DC, would be the city to attack.

He had heard the Americans say, "*Cut off the head of the snake and the snake dies.*"

Washington, DC was the head of the snake. He would kill hundreds of thousands by poisoning their water.

After Tarik detailed his plan, his chief scientist spoke up.

"You will not get the concentration of the poison required by spraying it over the water given the small amounts that UAVs can carry. However, we have something you may be interested in.

"We have discovered how to infuse the poison into a special foam and cover it with a durable plastic shell. We will mold the body and wings of the UAV with this plastic-covered foam. The UAV will be safe to handle with gloves, but the plastic covering will dissolve quickly when in contact with water, releasing the poison."

Tarik smiled as he envisioned the widespread terror that method of delivery would create.

"How do we get the UAVs close to the water source?" he asked, as he placed large overhead photos on the table. The photos showed the three main bodies of water used for drinking in Washington, DC.

"How big are these UAVs?" asked Ahmed.

"The wings are about a half meter long, and the body is a bit shorter in length," answered the scientist.

"How many will you need?" Ahmed asked, while reviewing the large photos.

"To achieve the highest lethality, we will need approximately eighteen per water source."

Ahmed jabbed the photo with his finger. Tarik and the scientist looked at what he was indicating.

"Communication towers," Ahmed said. "See these covered antennas? We can place our little birds inside those and wait for the launch signal, sending them all out at once."

Tarik scanned the photos quickly and said, "There are no towers close to the water sources."

"Then build them," was Ahmed's simple answer, as he pointed at the vacant ground in close proximity to each source of the city's drinking water.

Yes, of course, I have the contacts in DC to cut through the red tape. I could have them built quickly. The communication towers would be modern-day Trojan Horses, Tarik thought.

"How long will it take you to build and test these UAVs?" he asked the scientist.

"About three months."

"You have two."

The scientist nodded.

CHAPTER 34

At the hospital, Dave asked Sheriff Dayton to call Jackson Baer.

Jax brought the cavalry.

Scott and eight of his operators converged on the hospital and set up a tight security bubble around Dave and Jax. Scott still had Lydia with him. Jax had instructed him to not let the girl out of his sight. He took that as a direct order, and he was very good at following orders.

Lydia's head was reeling as she seemed to tumble from one crisis to another.

In the last two days, she had seen a guy stabbed to death, been chased by men with radios and guns, seen a mind-blowing computer set up, been kidnapped, whacked a psycho bitch in the head who was trying to electrocute her, escaped from captivity, flirted with a college boy, hacked a database, and was picked up by a for-real tough guy.

She and the tough guy had just raced across town to the hospital to help the man whom she had randomly sat beside in the park, and who had probably saved her life by getting her away from the people who wanted the briefcase back.

137

Scott flashed his brilliant white teeth at the nurses with a running litany of, "Hey, how ya' doing? How's it going? Good to see ya!" as he smoothly and continuously maneuvered his way to Dave's room.

He made sure that Lydia stayed in close proximity at his eight o'clock. That positioning allowed him to push her out of harm's way if necessary with his left hand, while drawing his pistol with his right.

Scott's head moved slowly from side to side, checking each door and opening before he passed it, looking for threats. He appeared calm, but his heart jackhammered and adrenaline created a metallic taste in his mouth—a feeling he knew all too well when charging toward the unknown.

Twice, Lydia noticed him sweep his jacket to the rear as he placed his right hand on the grip of his pistol. Both times, his movement was smooth and quick with no more effort than if he was inhaling or exhaling. She could tell that as soon as he was certain there was no danger, his hand moved away, allowing his jacket to cover the weapon.

She walked quickly, determined to keep up with him. There was no fucking way anyone else was going to grab her again.

As they entered Dave's room, Scott stopped short and eyeballed the sheriff, as if trying to determine if he was the real thing or not. They looked like two dogs eyeing the same fire hydrant.

Jax broke the stand-off saying, "Scott, glad you're here."

Dave was sitting up in bed. He looked at Lydia and asked, "Are you okay?"

"Well, I'm here," she replied.

"Quite a couple of days, huh?"

"Uh, well it hasn't exactly been a *normal* couple of days for me. Is this normal for you?"

"It's a little abnormal for me, as well," he said.

"What happened to you?" she asked.

"I was in a little traffic accident."

The sheriff snorted at that and rolled his eyes.

"Did they hurt you?" Dave asked.

"No, but I'm pretty sure I left a tattoo on the bitch who was supposed to keep me locked up." Lydia grinned just a little. In spite of all the crap that had happened in the past two days, Dave enjoyed seeing her express an emotion other than fear.

"Let's get out of here," Dave stated.

"I'm not sure you're ready for that," Jax replied.

"Yes, I am. We've got work to do."

"What work to do?" Sheriff Dayton asked.

"I've got to buy a new truck," Dave deadpanned, without a hint of sarcasm.

"Dave, I'll need you to come by the station tomorrow to give a statement."

"I will. I'll be there."

"I'm trusting you. I could hold you as a material witness."

Dave looked the sheriff in the eye.

"I'll be there, Tom."

Sheriff Dayton looked skeptical even as he nodded.

The hospital staff stubbornly demanded that Dave be transported from his room in a wheelchair. Dave finally relented, grumbling the entire trip to the double door entrance. Scott, with Lydia trailing behind, provided security for Dave's move from the room to the vehicle.

Jax had already pulled his truck under the canopy at the entrance.

Dave groaned in pain as Jax helped him out of the wheelchair and into his truck.

"Okay, I know you've already got a plan forming," Jax said as they pulled out of the parking lot with Scott and Lydia following.

"We need to get the Wizard on this. We need intel. We need to hit these guys before they come at us again. They seem desperate and desperate men are dangerous. They're unpredictable and reckless. We can use that against them."

"If the people on that USB drive are really the ones involved, we will have to go to the DNI," Jax said.

Dave looked over at his friend and solemnly nodded.

CHAPTER 35

Dave, Jax, Lydia and Scott arrived at a safe house on the outskirts of Herndon, Virginia. A security team, tasked by Jax, was already in place and had the grounds surrounded.

"Lydia, you need to stay with us for a while. I'm concerned for your safety," Dave said softly as they entered the house.

"You couldn't get me out of here at gunpoint," she replied. Looking around at all the men with guns, she said, "Well, maybe you could, but I'm not going anywhere until you tell me what's going on."

"We'll know more tomorrow after we see the Wizard. There are pieces of this puzzle that don't fit. There's food in the kitchen; let's eat and get some rest. We'll leave early in the morning," Dave answered.

Lydia looked down at her bloodstained dress. "I need clothes."

"There's women's clothing in the closet of your bedroom. It's down the hall, second door on the right," replied Scott.

"Does the door lock?" Lydia asked.

"Only from the inside," Scott chuckled.

Lydia wasn't smiling.

"There are sandwiches on the kitchen counter. Grab one on the way up," he said as she left.

Lydia picked up one of the white boxed lunches and a can of Mountain Dew and took it to her room. She went in, locked the door, and looked around. Not bad. Nice stuff . . . certainly better than the women's shelter and much better than the futon she had been sleeping on at Angela's.

She checked out the closet. There was women's clothing in it, all right—if you were a fifty-year-old office worker. She shook her head and closed the closet. Looking through the dresser drawers, she found a large Washington Nationals T-shirt.

Her room had its own bathroom. She wasn't sure she had ever stayed in a room that had its own bathroom, other than a hotel room. She turned on the shower, kicked off her Vans, and dropped her bloodied dress and underwear in a pile. She ducked under the steaming water and it felt amazing.

So, this must be how rich people live: lots of hot water and privacy.

There was a bottle of shampoo in the shower. She washed her hair twice.

After twenty minutes of uninterrupted hot water, she turned off the faucets, stepped out of the shower and used one of the fresh-smelling, fluffy towels to wrap her wet hair. She used another one to dry off. *This is quite luxurious living—two towels, both clean at the same time.*

Lydia pulled the heavy t-shirt on and continued rubbing her hair with the towel.

She sat on the edge of the bed, opened the boxed lunch, and ate the turkey sandwich in about six bites. She followed that with a long swallow of the Mountain Dew. It was cold, and the bubbles seemed to clean the day's grime from her throat.

She didn't remember falling asleep.

She awoke to a knock on her door. The lights were still on in her room, the sandwich wrapper was on the bed, and her unfinished drink was on the bedside table. She could hear Scott calling through the door.

"Lydia, we're leaving in thirty minutes. You up?"

"Yeah. Yeah, I'm up. I'll be ready."

She looked at the clock on the table beside the bed. It was 7 a.m. She'd been asleep for nine hours.

Whoa, that was weird. I must have been really tired.

She dragged herself out of bed and washed her face with cold water.

Her hair stuck out in every direction, the aftermath of going to sleep with it still damp. She found a brush and tried to run it through, but her hair was tangled beyond help. Using the palms of her hands, she smoothed it down as much as possible.

Lydia removed the T-shirt and put her dirty clothes back on.

The three men were sitting around the kitchen table, having coffee. They didn't look much better than she felt. They all must have stayed up late. They had the same clothes on that they'd been wearing the previous night.

Dave offered her a coffee in a Styrofoam cup.

"Let's get something to eat," Scott said.

They left in the two trucks, stopping at a truck stop about ten minutes from the house and blending right in with the rough, truck-stop crowd. Squeezing into a booth, Dave and Jax sat on one side, Scott and Lydia on the other. They all ordered coffees.

Dave and Jax then ordered ham and eggs; Scott, a veggie omelet. Lydia ordered eggs over easy, ham, hash browns, biscuits, a waffle, a side of bacon, and a large glass of orange juice. All three men stared at her for a second: she had ordered breakfast like a linebacker.

"What? I'm hungry!" she said defensively.

They hid their smiles behind their upraised coffee mugs.

The men finished their breakfast and Lydia sighed as she turned up the last of her orange juice.

"That was good!" she said.

Dave paid the check, leaving a larger tip than was required. As they walked across the parking lot, Lydia said to Scott, "I've got to get something to wear. I can't wear this guy's blood another day."

"You're right. Stand by." He called Dave in the other truck. They spoke briefly and Scott looked at Lydia. "Do you know where a clothing store is?"

"Give me your phone," she said.

She rapidly tapped the screen with her thumbs and returned the phone. She told Scott to follow the directions in Google Maps. He looked at his screen and saw that the destination was only two miles away.

"Okay." He called Dave and gave him the destination. Jax slowed, allowing Scott to lead.

The directions Lydia had entered led them to a Goodwill store.

"Is this it?" Scott questioned, as he pulled into the parking lot. Jax parked behind him.

"Yep," she answered.

"Go to Jax's truck first," he instructed.

She walked back to the passenger's side of Jax's vehicle and Dave buzzed the window down. "We'll be behind the store. Scott will be where he is now. If anything happens in there, run away from the threat. Run to us in the back, or to Scott in the front, understand?"

"Yes."

"Here, use this." He handed her two one-hundred-dollar bills.

She looked at the bills and back at Dave.

Obviously, he had never shopped at Goodwill. She could buy half the store for two hundred dollars. Lydia took the money and walked into the store.

She emerged twenty minutes later wearing a Pink Floyd, tie-dyed T-shirt over black jeans. She had on black moto boots, an olive-drab Army jacket, and a cable-knit beanie. A large crochet bag was slung over her shoulder.

"Nice," was all Scott said, as Lydia climbed into the truck. He drove around back to where Jax was parked. Lydia stepped out of the truck and dropped her old clothes in the dumpster. She walked over and passed one hundred and thirty-three dollars in change through the window to Dave. Dave and Jax exchanged raised eyebrows as Dave folded the money into his pocket.

CHAPTER 36

Dave, Jax, and Lydia arrived at the Wizard's place. Jax badged them in.

The Wiz took one look at Lydia in her new clothes and felt like he had around girls in middle school—unsure of himself and self-conscious. He wiped his sweaty palms on his pants.

Lydia, speaking to Dave and Jax with an edge to her voice, asked, "One of you smart guys want to tell me why we're back at hacking central, and what's going on?"

Jax said, "We may as well tell her. She's not exactly unwitting any longer."

Dave made eye contact with Lydia. She didn't blink or look away.

"You are what's known as an outlier: a variable outside the equation. You were never supposed to be involved in this, and there were no contingency plans for you; that's one of the reasons you're still alive. The people trying to find you aren't sure if you were the dead man's contact," Dave explained. "They couldn't believe that you were totally random. As for me, I'm known to them, but you meeting me by chance confused them even more."

"Who are those *people?*" Lydia asked.

146

"Some politicians, former military officers, and a defense contractor," Dave continued. "They've been using the wars and money from selling diverted military goods to buy mineral rights in Iraq and Afghanistan and it's made them a lot of money. The details of who is involved, the amounts, and the location of the money are on the USB drive the man smuggled out of the office in his briefcase. The men in that group want that USB drive back."

"Can't you just call the cops?" she asked.

"No. No cops. This is a government problem, not a law enforcement problem. The cops are not equipped to handle something like this. This has to be handled in-house. Government to government," Jax explained.

Jax looked at the Wizard and said, "I want to know everything there is to know about these guys."

"I've been working it for two days," the Wiz replied. "Here's what I have so far: the ringleader is none other than Warren Battles, Deputy Director of National Intelligence."

The Wizard looked over at Dave, as he knew that Battles had been Dave's boss for the last five years before he retired.

The Wiz continued. "Mike Davis, retired Air Force Three-Star General who owns International Solutions, is also involved. I can't believe the FBI hasn't been knocking at his door. In the last four years of his military career, he earned the congressional set limit of 168,000 dollars a year. However, the year he retired, he started International Solutions as a sole proprietorship. His startup costs to purchase land, staff up, buy training vehicles, weapons and equipment had to be in the neighborhood of five million dollars. I can't find any evidence that he borrowed a penny.

"Allen Greensmith, Secretary of Defense, and Foster Hillum, the CEO of a huge defense manufacturing firm, are the other two members. It looks like they have booked the value of the mineral rights at around 500 million dollars. That's way overvalued, but they do have cash on hand, in several accounts, amounting to 120 million dollars. That's real money, not projected value."

Dave looked at Jax. "Ideas?" he asked.

Jax asked the Wiz, "Were you able to do what I asked?"

"Yep. First, I set up a surge account, a central depository for the money. Then I hacked into each of the accounts where they deposited funds and made myself a co-signer. I altered the algorithm they use to transfer money.

"Whenever they transfer funds from one account to another, they will see the money leaving their account. But instead of their intended destination, it will go to the surge account I set up. That surge account automatically empties when it reaches a one-million-dollar balance.

"It will transfer that one million dollars to smaller accounts I've hidden in other countries. They will see the funds leave their account and a corresponding balance will show up in their destination account. However, the balance they see will be a mirror image of the money in the account I set up: a ghost account. They will not be able to withdraw the funds from their new accounts because it will never actually be there."

"How long before they figure that out?" asked Dave.

"It depends on how good they are. I have tripwires set to let me know every time they attempt a transaction. If they start acting weird, I'll execute a script that will empty all of their accounts immediately. It could take days or weeks before they realize they actually don't have any money."

"Holy crap! That's some next-level shit! Did you come up with that plan? You've *got* to show me how to do that!" Lydia exclaimed.

The Wizard blushed.

"For now, we know more about them than they know about us. That's good, but we've got some work to do to neutralize their efforts," Jax said.

"They murdered Miranda, Jax. We're not going to *neutralize their efforts*. We're going to kill every single one of the bastards," Dave spat.

"I understand. First, we get some backing. We need sanctions for this. That's how we operate," Jax replied.

Dave narrowed his eyes at Jax.

"In this country, anyway," Jax offered.

CHAPTER 37

THREE MONTHS EARLIER

"Mr. Battles, Mr. Marshall is on line one."

Warren Battles picked up the phone. "Warren Battles."

"Mr. Battles, how are you?" Tarik said.

"I'm well, Mr. Marshall, and you?" Battles answered as he began the clandestine dance with the man most responsible for his mega wealth.

"I'm in town and wondered if you were available for dinner."

"Of course. Where would you like to meet?"

"The Greek restaurant, Komi, on 17th Street?" Tarik suggested.

"Perfect. I know the place. Eight p.m.?"

"Yes. I'll see you then," Tarik said.

Tarik arrived thirty minutes early, as he always did. He felt it gave him a tactical advantage.

He planned every meeting as if it was a military exercise. He checked the delivery entrance in the back as he drove around the block, familiarizing himself with the area, looking for closed businesses or buildings should he need a quick escape and a place to hide.

Arriving early also allowed him to choose his seat at the table, giving him a view of the entrance and exit.

Tarik felt relatively safe in Washington, DC. It was amazing how a five-thousand-dollar suit and a chauffeured car guaranteed anonymity in this status-conscious town.

Battles arrived ten minutes late.

He strode across the room in his tailored, dark suit like he owned the place. His light blue French cuffs were extended precisely one-half inch from the sleeves of his suit jacket and his pink silk tie was knotted with a perfect, finger-sized dimple.

Over two cups of tea for Tarik and two cocktails for Battles, they exchanged the requisite pleasantries which both men abhorred. After they'd ordered their meal, Tarik opened the business conversation by asking Battles for assistance in securing permits to build three telecommunication towers in the Washington, DC area. He said he represented a large European company that needed the towers built as soon as possible. They needed someone to smooth the process and allow the towers to begin construction in less than thirty days.

Tarik's client was willing to pay a commission of 250,000 dollars for expediting each tower and an annual payment of 25,000 dollars per tower to the expediter.

The towers would be large and contain several microwave antennas.

Tarik assured Battles that the return his client received from leasing the towers would be well worth a finder's fee and annual payments.

Battles replied, "I should be able to help you obtain those permits in a timely manner."

"I was hoping you would," Tarik said. He removed a thick manila envelope from inside his jacket and slid it across the table. "This is an incentive payment of 50,000 dollars."

With a practiced move, Battles smoothly placed the envelope in his jacket.

During the remainder of the meal, Tarik forced himself to make small talk about the weather in Austria and the banking business, all the while thinking about how this greedy son-of-a-whore, Battles, would never get to spend a penny of the commissions.

Battles smiled appropriately during Tarik's monologue, all the while mentally calculating his fee for Tarik's proposed project.

750,000 dollars for acquiring the sites plus 75,000 dollars passive income a year for . . . well, forever. Easy money.

He could make that happen; he would make that happen. Battles thought how good it was to know wealthy businessmen who recognized his talents and were willing to pay him to get things done.

Tarik paid the check. The two men stood up, shook hands, and departed.

A light mist blanketed the sky. Puddles formed on the sidewalks.

On the way to his town car, head bowed with the collar of his raincoat turned up, Battles hit speed dial and placed a call. "Can you meet me in an hour?" he asked.

"An hour? I had dinner plans." Mona's apologetic answer was met with stony silence.

"... but I can cancel them," she added.

"The regular place," Battles said, and then disconnected without a goodbye.

Making money always made him horny.

CHAPTER 38

Battles arrived at the historic Hay-Adams Hotel and stopped by the bar to get a double scotch, neat.

The manager of the hotel was indebted to Battles for using his political power to untangle an immigration action that would have sent him back to Jordan, and possibly a firing squad.

Because of that, Battles could get one of the luxury suites with just a phone call and no advance notice.

He never slept there. He only used the room several times a month, usually with Mona Solano. Occasionally, he occupied it when one of his newest interns was hoping to find favor with her boss.

Once inside the suite, Battles poured two fingers of complimentary Glenlivet into a heavy tumbler. He turned off all the lights, except one lamp near the bed, and opened both French doors to the balcony, allowing the sheer curtains to flutter in the warm spring air. The view of the White House and the Washington Monument was magnificent as both shimmered in the light rain against a black night sky.

Battles sat on one of the richly upholstered wing-back chairs, loosened his tie and lifted his glass as he intoned his favorite toast, "It's good to be king!"

He had left the door ajar and did not bother to get up as Mona came in. He motioned her over with his drink.

"Hi," she said.

"Over here," he said, patting his lap.

She set her purse and raincoat on the desk and came over to him.

Battles grabbed her around the waist and pulled her into his lap. He kissed her with his strong alcohol breath.

"I haven't heard from you in a while," she said, pulling back and watching his face for signs that he might explode and begin yelling at her, as had happened before.

"Yeah, I've been busy keeping our country safe for democracy," he slurred.

Mona wasn't sure what she felt for Warren Battles. At first, their encounters had been very romantic; there had been rides around Washington, DC at night in his chauffeur-driven town car, dinners at the finest restaurants, and evenings at the Hay-Adams.

That had stopped almost two years ago. Now, he rarely called and the dinners and romantic car rides were almost non-existent. When he did call, it was always a booty call. She wasn't sure why she hung on to hope for the relationship.

True, she was attracted to powerful men. After all, she worked for one of the most powerful men in the country. Yet, when it came to Warren, she couldn't seem to help herself; she dropped everything and came running every time he called.

Battles began roughly squeezing her breasts as she sat on his lap. She started to unbutton her blouse when he grabbed it with both hands and tore the material, buttons popping off as he pushed it back over her shoulders.

Before she could protest, he pulled her bra up from underneath, exposing her breasts. He was rough as he sucked and bit her breasts. She began pushing her hands against his shoulders as he quickly stood up, almost launching her onto the floor.

Holding her wrists in a vice-like grip, he pushed her face over the edge of the bed. She felt her skirt being pushed up over her back as he yanked her panties down. White-hot pain shot through her as he forced himself into her.

He was a wild man, possessed. He slammed against her, driving her into the bed.

Tears rolled down her cheeks as he physically abused her and mentally tortured her.

Finally, he grunted and spasmed into her. He withdrew, turned, and walked to the bathroom without a word.

Mona slowly pushed herself up and off the bed and pulled her panties back on. She was sore and nauseous as she tried to pull the shreds of her blouse around her.

She heard the shower running as she put her raincoat on, fumbled with the top button, and left. Mona kept her head down, averting her eyes from the bright lights of the hallway that only served to illuminate her shame.

CHAPTER 39

Battles had bullied his way through all the red tape.

Less than two weeks after their dinner, he had the two plots of land Tarik had selected tied up in fifty-year leases, calling in favors and threatening blackmail to avoid lengthy FCC hearings.

Before the neighbors knew construction-sites were being considered, the ground was cleared, concrete footings poured, and steel structures were rising in the air. He exerted the same bullying force when securing a hospital rooftop site for one of the towers. The upshot was that the towers would be up and operational before neighbors could get any traction to try and stop them.

By then, Battles would have been paid his commission of seven hundred and fifty thousand dollars, and Tarik and his clients could fight the community.

The tower construction went quickly. Less than ninety days from their meeting at the Greek restaurant, workmen were securing huge, ten-foot circular dish antennas to the sides of the two hundred and fifty foot red and white spires.

***

157

Tarik had also been busy.

His scientists had mastered the fabrication of the foam and plastic that they intended to saturate with Sarin. Weeks of testing had proven the concept both reliable and deadly.

For testing, they made several cubes the size of dice. They'd impregnated the foam with a drop of Sarin the size of a pinhead and sealed the cube with the dissolvable plastic. They placed the innocuous-looking cube beside a rabbit's cage in the laboratory's hermetically sealed room.

Nothing happened until some water was sprayed on the cube. Once wet, the plastic dissolved quickly, allowing the Sarin to gas-off, killing the rabbit in minutes. They also experimented with dropping the cube in a rabbit's water bowl. One drink, and the same results for the rabbit.

Once the method of delivery was proven, the engineers turned their attention to shaping the specialized foam into the body and wings of the UAVs. The wings were about one-half-meter long, the body of the aircraft about a quarter meter. A high-torque electric motor and high-capacity battery would power the UAV to its destination. The plan was to install six of the UAVs into the covered parabolic dish antennas that resembled a huge, deep-dish pizza pan. They would put three dishes on each tower.

They built a rack that would hold the UAVs and keep them plugged into a power source to keep the batteries charged and their small computerized brains alive. Upon signal, the ten-foot diameter cover would blow off the three-foot-deep antenna. After four minutes of warm-up and GPS alignment time, the little birds would be pushed out of their "nest." Their navigation system was preprogrammed to fly directly to the closest municipal water supply and crash into it. There, the special covering over the plastic and foam body would dissolve, releasing the Sarin poison into the water.

Sarin has beautifully horrific properties, which means that it is just as deadly on contact with the skin as it is if taken internally.

In his mind, Tarik visualized thousands of American infidels writhing in the streets and hospitals overflowing; the twenty-four-hour cable news coverage would stampede the rest of the nation into sheer panic. The terror of the unknown is always much worse than the actual event. And this event would be nightmarish.

America was too large to bomb into submission, but twenty-four-hour news coverage could scare the country into inaction and uncertainty. *Paralysis by analysis*—Tarik would cause paralysis that would wreak havoc on the financial markets, and every other sector of the country.

If the nation's food or water supply became questionable, anarchy would reign and American society would break down into a free-fire zone. Since Americans owned over three hundred million guns, Tarik knew Americans would not hesitate to liberally use those weapons against one another in the name of survival. He knew that the only way to kill a population the size of America's was to set in motion events that would make it self-destruct.

Tarik intended to do just that.

CHAPTER 40

"Show me how you set up the fake transfers?" Lydia asked the Wiz.

"I got the idea from a con man named Frank Abagnale. He had a con going, back when people actually went into banks to make deposits using the banks' preprinted deposit slips.

Abagnale printed deposit slips with the banks' names on them, but added his own account number that was read by the banks' new computers, across the bottom.

"He went to several banks and replaced the official bank deposit slips with his own. So, no matter what the customer hand wrote into the account line, the computer read his script and deposited the money into Abagnale's account. I did the same scam, but with code. No matter where the owners of the money try to send it, it goes to my account."

"How much so far?"

"About fifty million," Wiz replied. "They are slowly moving the money, but haven't panicked yet. They think they're being careful. They have no idea it's already too late."

"Will they figure it out?"

"Yes, eventually, but not soon enough—and there will be no fingerprints. The money will just be gone."

"Oh my God! That's really scary. Do you do stuff like that all the time?"

"No, just when ordered to. I have to be very careful or they'll send me back." The Wizard immediately wished that he could put that last sentence back in his mouth.

"Back where?" Lydia asked.

"Uh, back to jail. That's where they found me. I wasn't there long, and I wouldn't have lasted long there. I'm not exactly jail material," he said.

"So, do you hack?" Wiz asked, trying to deflect any further inquiries along those lines.

"Some. I'm comfortable with what I know, but I haven't had a lot of opportunities. So, how did you find the accounts in the first place?" Lydia asked.

The Wiz remembered that she had been kidnapped before he'd found the information on the USB drive.

"It was on the USB drive you and Dave brought here," he said.

"Do you still have it?"

"No, it burned in Dave's house. I cloned it before I attempted to open it, just in case I missed a virus that would destroy the contents of the drive."

"Wait, his house burned?"

"Yeah, the guys looking for the USB drive broke in, killed his housekeeper, and burned his house."

Lydia went very quiet at the news. "He never mentioned that."

"I'm not surprised; that guy is pretty closed off. Sometimes he scares me, but he's the guy you want around if the shit hits the fan."

"Yeah, I can see that," she said. "Show me what the files on the drive look like."

Wiz moved to an isolated computer and quickly clicked the keys, opening the spreadsheets. He ran his finger down the screen and pointed.

"Here are their names. See how the funds have been equally divided at every sale, and see where it all started almost eleven years ago? They are equal partners, and equally complicit."

The rows were divided by columns that were headed by dates of deposits.

"Hey, scroll back over to the right side for a second . . . see these numbers?" She pointed to a single deposit to Warren Battles for $750,000. "None of the others have that deposit."

The Wizard looked closely at the screen, then up at her.

"You're right. I was so focused on the big money that I missed that."

"What is he getting paid for that the others are not?" she asked.

"Let's check," he said. The Wiz went back to his main computer console and began opening screen after screen. Lydia could tell he was browsing through bank records. Finally, she saw *Ariana Consulting Company* across the top of a bank statement.

Wiz told her, "This is one of Battles's shell companies. He's not very good at hiding his business; I found this within an hour of data mining him. He used the phone number from one of his vacation houses for the fictitious corporation number. It was sloppy tradecraft."

"It looks like there was only one deposit," Lydia said, while leaning over his shoulder to get a better view of the screen.

The Wizard could smell the shampoo she'd used. He was afraid to speak or move—afraid to break this spell. At this particular instant, he couldn't care less about Warren Battles. His mind had been effectively neutralized by Lydia's presence and he was only interested in the beautiful, smart girl standing within inches of him.

He was impressed that she had suggested he cross-check Battles's account to determine where the $750,000 came from. He knew to always *follow the money*, but at the moment, that very basic concept had completely evaded him, while another, more instinctive concept completely captivated him.

"Uh, right, let's check that," he managed to croak out.

He pulled up a scanned copy of the canceled check. It was drawn on an Austrian Bank by a company named Premier Communications Concepts. A search of international databases revealed Premier Communication Concept was founded only four months ago in Bern, Switzerland. Digging further, he determined that it must be a shell company because there was no meat on the company's bones. A very one-dimensional webpage looked to have been cloned from a legitimate communication company.

The Wiz began a specialized search comparing text and script. Within minutes, he found the original webpage. It belonged to a huge international communication tower builder and owner. They owned over 35,000 towers in the US alone. The script was copied and pasted into the Premier Communication Concept webpage.

He then searched US leases for towers held by Premier Communication Concept.

There were only three of them, all in Washington, DC.

One was near the Capitol at the Tidal Basin, one was located in Georgetown, near the Potomac River, and the third stood atop the Children's National Hospital.

He searched the Federal Communication Commission databases and could find no record of hearings to justify the construction of the towers.

"This is odd," he said. "I can't find any leases from any of the communication companies to lease space on these towers. It says here that usually those leases are in place before the towers are built. The leases are the driving force for both the location and the construction of the tower. There has to be a demand before they build those things."

"Can you give me access to the Internet?" Lydia asked.

"This is a classified system running one-of-a-kind software," he began protesting.

"I just need an Internet feed," she said in a low voice while locking eyes with him.

"Oh, yes, of course, I have that," he offered, completely helpless to resist her.

Meanwhile, Dave and Jax had wandered into the comm center and were quietly observing from across the room.

Wiz pointed to a laptop isolated at a stand-alone workstation. "That one . . . you can use that one," he said.

She pulled a chair up to the desk and began typing on the laptop. The Wiz watched her typing speed for only a minute and then glanced over at Dave and Jax. They both grinned at his blatant surprise at Lydia's keyboarding skills. After only a couple of minutes, she said, "Look at this: something's not right."

The Wiz joined in, "The owners are Premier Communication Concept. Those towers and the hospital tower went up at the same time, about four months ago." The Wiz leaned over her, hit a DVI switch, and put an overhead shot of each tower, side by side, on the big screen that dominated his communication center. On seeing them all together, it was obvious that they were of the same construction. In fact, they looked like they'd been cut out with a cookie cutter.

"Wait," he said as he rolled his chair back in front of his keyboard and typed furiously. Photos of similar towers began filling one of the other six-foot screens on the wall. "Look at these. None are the same—similar, but not the same. There's different orientation of the dish antennas, different angles, different numbers of antennas."

Jax added, "The size and orientation of the antennas are dependent on what they're relaying or transmitting. Microwave antennas are generally pointed to an adjoining tower, sometimes thirty or more miles away as they relay communication data to the next one in line. So, what I'm saying is that they shouldn't be exactly the same. However, those type of antennas are no longer in use; microwave has been replaced by fiber optics."

"But all of these are new, and all of these are exactly the same," Lydia said.

As if suddenly being able to make out the picture-in-a-picture of a stereogram, the men saw what she was already seeing. And she was right: the three new towers were identical.

"Where are those towers?" Jax asked.

She pulled up another screen. "Google Earth," she said. She dropped pins on the map indicating the three Premier Communication Concept tower leases.

She zoomed in on the image to reveal a tower construction site near the Tidal Basin. Moving the cursor over to the site in Georgetown near the Potomac River, she found a second site. The roof of the Children's National Hospital held the third tower.

Each of the tall red and white structures had three, huge, drum-like antennas attached to their sides.

CHAPTER 41

Once he'd moved out of the Shaw neighborhood, life was pretty tame for thirteen-year-old Levon Mitchell.

His Nana had taken him out of the tough northwest DC area and away from the gangs. Levon tried to tell his Nana that there weren't any "gangs" in Shaw, just "crews." She said they were the same thing and that she knew about the "crew" who was trying to recruit him.

The KDP, named after the Kennedy Playground, was both territorial and deadly. Last summer, a KDP crew member shot through a chain-link fence, killing a kid from the next neighborhood over just for being from the next neighborhood over.

Nana was a housekeeper at the Children's National Hospital. She was frugal and strong-willed. She'd managed to buy a small three-room house ten blocks from the hospital.

Levon was a naturally talented artist.

On Saturdays, he went with his Nana to the hospital and roamed the halls, exploring and sketching the activity of the doctors and nursing staff. Occasionally, he would go across the parking lot to McMillan Reservoir and sketch the wildlife in the park.

Levon enjoyed watching the men hang the huge dish antennas on the tower that was under construction on the roof of the hospital. He liked the way the workers seemed to have a purpose. He enjoyed seeing the progress each week and watching something being built up instead of being torn down.

Maybe he could design buildings and have people build them . . . he was unsure if that was his dream or his escape plan.

Each Saturday, he sat on a bench, looked up at the roof, and sketched the tower in its different phases of construction. He hung the drawings on the wall in his bedroom. His drawings were detailed and to scale, indicating mature talent for the young artist.

Levon stood now in the hospital parking lot watching the dark clouds build on the horizon as the huge crane lifted a ten-foot, cylinder-shaped object up the side of the tower. Two of the construction workers were attached three-quarters of the way up the structure by their harnesses. They were using hand tools to secure the containers to the tower. The wind was picking up, and one of the climber's helmets blew off.

Levon jumped as the huge, drum-shaped container hanging from the crane's cable banged into the side of the tower. Even from the ground, he could see that the impact had put a small dent in the edge of the container.

The man attached to the tower quickly looked at the damage. He motioned to the crane operator by circling his hand over his head to continue raising the container. The rain began just as they finished attaching the container to the structure. The two men quickly climbed down and the workers left. Levon ran back inside the hospital to avoid the downpour.

On one of his hospital explorations, Levon had discovered a door to the roof. He waited until the brief, but intense rain shower subsided and then climbed the steps. As he pushed through the rooftop access door, he unknowingly triggered a silent alarm. He crossed the roof, squeezed through a narrow gap in the construction fence, and walked under the massive structure. He looked straight up at the towering spire and was motivated to sketch it from that perspective.

Looking down to make sure he was directly in the center of the four legs of the tower, he noticed a small piece of black plastic lying in a puddle at his feet. Levon picked up the piece of plastic and turned it over in his hand. It looked like it had broken off of something. He remembered the big cylinder banging into the tower. He looked up and saw a small tear in the cover of the cylinder. Discarding the piece of plastic, he began to sketch on his drawing pad.

Just then, the roof door opened and a security guard yelled at him, "Hey, kid! Get out of there! You're not allowed up here!"

Without warning, Levon pitched forward and vomited explosively. He couldn't seem to catch his breath as he fell to his knees. The last thing he remembered was falling face-first into a pool of his own vomit.

CHAPTER 42

The Wiz and Lydia were on a mission to explain why these three identical towers would differ from other towers, hoping to explain their intended use. They decided that researching the permits would give them the type of antennas designated for the towers.

Lydia was searching local news postings for *communication towers* and *communication tower permitting,* while the Wiz researched the permitting process. She found a couple of area blogs and news articles expressing outrage; the consensus was that the towers were a blight on the skyline and should not have been allowed to be built. Ironically, the very towers being complained about were the same type transmitting the indignant ravings across the Internet.

Lydia also came across an editorial piece in *The Washington Post* written three days prior entitled, "Are the New Telecommunication Towers Safe?" The article described a thirteen-year-old boy who had become gravely ill while playing under a communication tower on top of the Children's National Hospital. *The Post* indicated that he'd ingested a chemical of some sort while on the roof near the base of the tower. The young man would likely have died had a security guard not found him and immediately transported him to the emergency room.

"Wiz, look at this," Lydia said, pointing to her screen.

"Okay. So?"

"It's one of the three towers. I think we should find out more about this."

"Why? It was probably just some kid who spilled paint or cleaning fluid on himself that he could have been trying to steal to get high."

"I don't know . . . something seems off about this. The article said he had a sketch pad with him. I've never known a huffer to bring a sketch pad along on a break-in," she said.

"Let me see if I can get the incident report." The Wiz sighed. In just a minute or two, the Wizard was prowling the hospital database. "Give me the date and the kid's name."

"Three days ago, and his name is . . . it's not listed," Lydia replied.

"I don't need it. Here it is. His name is Levon Mitchell. Thirteen years old. Here's his medical record; as of yesterday, he was still alive, but very sick. It says he ingested an unknown toxin that affected his nervous system. The ER doc was a former army doctor who recognized his symptoms as some kind of poisoning and gave him atropine. The kid responded well, but he's still on a ventilator. It says here that the doc sent blood and urine samples to the CDC. Okay, that last part's weird."

Dave and Jax entered the room. Dave, looking over the two data miners' shoulders, weighed in, "That's all fascinating, but what does that have to do with the guys we're looking at?"

"Battles is tied to those towers, and this incident occurred at one of those towers," Lydia fired back.

Wiz nodded his head in agreement.

"But why are the towers important?" Dave questioned.

"Look, those tower permits are all wrong. Who spends that kind of money to build towers with no telecommunication leases, and why? The USB data shows that Battles was the only one who received money for the tower permit process. If we can find that Battles is using his government position to bully these permits through, you may have the leverage to open an investigation into his financial dealings," the Wiz replied.

"We need to go to the hospital and check out that tower," Lydia said with finality as she stared down the two men. "What?" she asked, looking back and forth between Dave and Jax, who stood there with their arms folded.

"You certainly aren't the scared young lady I met on a park bench a few days ago," Dave observed.

"I was having a bad day," was all Lydia said.

CHAPTER 43

Children's National Medical Center is recognized as one of the United States' best pediatric care providers. The 300-bed hospital is located adjacent to the McMillan Reservoir and Howard University in Washington, DC.

They all sat in Jax's truck in the parking lot of the hospital.

"Okay, so here's our play," Lydia began, as if she was involved in an *Ocean's Eleven* plot. "I'll pretend I'm a reporter and go in and interview the kid's parents. I'll talk to the doctor and maybe a nurse or two," she said, excitedly laying out her plan.

"Wait, I may have a better idea," Jax interrupted, holding his index finger in the air. He pulled out his phone, scrolled through his contacts, and tapped the number to connect.

"Chopper?" Jax asked the person on the other end of the phone call. After a brief conversation, Jax responded, "Well, we could meet you now. We're in the parking lot. See you in five."

"Who was that?" asked Wiz.

"The young man's attending physician, Dr. Bobby Alvarez. He started out in Iraq and completed his military service as the chief of the ER unit at the Role 3 in

Kandahar. Being a surgeon, he was, of course, given the nickname, *Chopper.*"

"How did you know he was the kid's doctor?" Lydia asked.

"I didn't, but when you said Children's National, I knew Bobby was a doc there, so I called him. Turns out he was on call the day they brought the kid in. Let's go," Jax said, as he got out of the truck.

They met Dr. Alvarez in the cafeteria and found a corner table that provided a little privacy.

"Bobby, you remember Dave. And this is Lydia and Tom."

Lydia turned just slightly, looked at *Tom*, and raised one eyebrow at discovering the Wizard actually had a real name.

"Hi, guys. Good to see you again, Dave."

"Good to see you too," Dave replied.

Turning to Jax, the doctor said, "Because you and Dave are here, I'm getting some sort of federal vibe."

"We're following up on an inquiry pushed to our office," Jax said. "What can you tell us about the incident involving the kid on the roof last Saturday?"

"There are HIPAA rules, but I can talk generalities." After a short pause, Bobby resumed. "It was a weird one—the kid presented just like the chemical warfare cases I saw in Iraq. But that's not possible for two reasons. First, it was isolated; he was the only patient. Second, he was on the roof of a hospital when it happened and not in some meth lab.

"Chem warfare poisoning victims usually have difficulty breathing, along with convulsions and tremors. The standard protocol is to hit them with atropine, so I used that on the kid. It knocked his symptoms down in a hurry. I also took blood and urine samples and sent them to the CDC."

The doctor's narrative confirmed what the Wiz had read in the chart he hacked earlier in the day.

"Why did you send samples to the CDC?" asked Jax.

"I had an odd feeling about this one that I'm not ready to talk about yet; I need some verification first. There's not much more I can tell you at this time."

"Thanks, Chopper. Will you let me know what you hear back from the CDC?" Jax asked.

Bobby Alvarez nodded his agreement just as his pager beeped. He pulled it from the pocket of his starched white coat and looked at the number. "Looks like I'm needed in the ER.

Jax, Dave . . . good to see you again. Let's get together for dinner soon. Good to meet you guys, too," he said to the Wiz and Lydia as he left the cafeteria and disappeared down the hall.

They went out the back door of the cafeteria and looked up at the huge red and white tower on the roof of the hospital. It could well have been an obelisk to the telecommunications gods.

"Let's go up and take a closer look," Dave said.

They took the stairs to the roof.

As the door was propped open, the alarm must have been disabled—probably for easy entry and exit by the construction crew; however, it was lunchtime and no workers were present. The tower was cordoned off with a padlocked personnel gate. They stood at the fence line and examined the massive steel structure.

"How does it work?" Lydia asked.

The Wizard launched into an explanation. "The operating principle of a parabolic antenna is that a point source of radio waves, at the focal point in front of a paraboloidal reflector of conductive material, will be reflected into a collimated plane wave beam along the axis—"

"Hold it!" Lydia interrupted, her hand in mid-air like a traffic cop.

"I meant, how does it work without electricity? There are no generators or batteries or big black cables running up the inside of the tower, like in the pictures we saw online. So, how does it operate?" she asked again.

"Well," he sputtered, "it can't work without power. I see what you mean now."

"Hey, they must have forgotten to lock the gate," Dave said, holding up the lock, but Lydia had watched him surreptitiously slide the lock pick he'd used on the briefcase back into his pocket.

The four of them walked across the roof to the concrete slab under the tower. It was almost completely bare, but there were still bits of construction debris lying around. Pieces of 2x4 lumber, with dried concrete on them, were stacked along one edge. Some rusty bolts lay in small puddles of water.

Almost dead center of the concrete slab, directly under the tower, was a small piece of shiny black plastic about the size of a dollar bill. The Wiz reached to pick it up, but Dave grabbed his shoulder and stopped him from touching it.

"Wait," Dave said. He looked around and found a plastic grocery bag that might have once contained one of the worker's lunches. Bringing the bag over, he used a rusty bolt to push the piece of plastic into the bag. He tied the top of the bag in a secure knot.

Without realizing it, Dave was standing in the same spot Levon had stood five days earlier. Dave looked up and saw the slight tear in the edge of the covering of the dish antenna. He pointed, showing the others the small, dark hole.

"Let's go," he said.

Back in the parking lot, Dave dropped the plastic piece—still wrapped in the grocery bag—into a Ziploc bag he found in Jax's truck. They quickly headed back to the safe house.

CHAPTER 44

Jax's cell phone rang early the next morning.

Unsure of what Battles and his group would try next, all four had stayed overnight at the safe house. Jax was fairly certain that Battles didn't know of his involvement with the USB drive, but he didn't want to take a chance on bringing violence to his home should they make a run at him. He was also not ready to involve his senior management at work.

He looked at the caller ID, saw it was Dr. Alverez, and answered the call with "Hey."

"I just got a call from the guys in Atlanta," Bobby said, referring to the CDC, but not wanting to say their name over the phone.

"And what merriment did they wish on you this morning?" Jax asked sarcastically.

"Golf Bravo," the doctor answered.

"Are they kidding?" Jax asked, suddenly deadly serious, not sure he believed what he was hearing.

"These guys *never* kid around. I think 'must not have a sense of humor' is one of the criteria for working there."

"Okay, thanks for the heads-up. Keep this close-hold and watch yourself. I'll give you a call if I find anything new," Jax promised.

Shit! Golf Bravo, coded using the phonic alphabet for GB, was the military identifier for Sarin. Sarin was possibly the most poisonous substance on earth. But if it was Sarin, how did the kid come in contact with it, and why wasn't he dead?

Following the smell of bacon, Jax walked to the kitchen and found Dave and Wiz sitting down for breakfast. Lydia was standing by the stove with her back to them. Apparently, Lydia was the cook this morning. He saw a plate set for him with two fried eggs and toast.

"I just got a call from Chopper. The CDC called back. They identified the toxin in the kid's blood. It's Sarin," he said.

"Sarin?" Dave asked. "How did he come in contact with Sarin in the middle of DC? That poison has been outlawed since 1997. There are no commercial uses of Sarin, and it's so poisonous that it's controlled like nuclear material."

"How poisonous is it?" asked the Wiz.

"It's twenty-six times more deadly than the cyanide gas used in gas chambers. A pinprick-sized drop is enough to kill a human," answered Dave, who had spent considerable time in Iraq chasing weapons of mass destruction.

"The Nazis developed it from a pesticide in 1938, but they found it too difficult to weaponize during World War II," he continued. "Every ounce of the world's production is accounted for, we hope. It's very fast-acting, so if the boy was exposed, he would have had a reaction to it within a minute or two. He had to have come in close contact with it near where the security guard found him."

"Under the tower," Lydia finished his thought.

All four of them slowly looked over at the used Ziploc pouch resting on the counter containing the cast-off grocery bag with the shiny, black, dollar-sized piece of plastic in it.

Dave was the first to say it: "Well, if that has Sarin on it, and it was leaking, we would already be dead."

"Wiz, how about finding us a glass jar with a really tight lid?" Jax suggested.

Wiz slid his chair away from the table, never taking his eyes off the Ziploc bag of death just in case it spontaneously exploded, contaminating them all. He returned from the garage bearing a one-gallon glass jar. He was wearing huge, yellow, dishwashing rubber gloves and a set of goggles foggy with perspiration. Despite the seriousness of the situation, it was all Lydia could do not to laugh at him.

"It had pickles in it. I poured them out and rinsed the jar out. Should I dry it?"

"Yes," said Dave. "Sarin is diluted by water, but can also be spread by water very easily."

The Wizard dried the jar, took a deep breath and held it before approaching the counter. He gently picked up the Ziploc and carefully placed it into the jar before tightly screwing the lid on as if he was trying to confine a cobra.

"I'm calling for an Ion Mobility Spectrometry team," Jax said.

An hour later, a white box truck backed up the drive. Two men got out and removed two large cases on wheels from the truck. Jax answered the door. As they entered, they looked back and forth between Jax and Dave.

"Are you the guys who ordered a dozen party clowns?" they asked with a straight face.

"Yes, we did, but since it's you two who showed up, I feel certain we'll get our money's worth," Jax retorted in the comfortable way soldiers joke when under stress. The men smiled.

They opened their cases and extracted blue hazmat suits and air tanks. They dressed carefully, checking each other's suits to ensure all the closures were sealed. Their air bottles hissed as they turned the valves on.

Jax motioned them into the kitchen and pointed at the glass jar.

The men approached the jar waving a wand attached to a box the size of a loaf of bread. No horns went off—so far, so good. Carefully picking up the pickle jar, they carried it to the truck, with Jax and Dave following behind. The truck contained a glass and metal box about four feet square and an array of dials, switches, and video screens. They unscrewed six big black knobs and opened one end of the box. They put the glass jar inside the box, closed the end, and screwed the knobs tightly against the frame.

The men began powering up their test equipment. Motors hummed as a vacuum seal was pulled inside the glass box to ensure there were no leaks. A green light on top of the box indicated a successful seal. The men gave a thumbs up to each other and removed their hazmat gear. For the first time since they'd suited up, one of the techs addressed Jax. "It's safe now. We'll test it on-site, as you instructed."

The other tech slid his arms into long rubber gloves that passed through the sealed glass wall, allowing him to manipulate the item to be tested without coming in contact with it. He unscrewed the lid of the jar and gently removed the plastic bags. Using a set of large plastic tweezers already inside the glass box, he carefully extracted the shiny black plastic part and set the piece on a stage the size of a hockey puck, illuminated by a bright spotlight.

Removing his hands from the long rubber gloves, he typed some commands on his keyboard. One of the computer monitors lit up with vertical lines in red, yellow, blue, and green that marched left to right across the screen. After a few minutes, he entered a command and the lines stopped moving.

"It's Sarin, sir," he said looking at Jax. "It's in very minute and diluted amounts, but it's definitely Sarin."

"Where did you find this?" the tech asked.

"On the roof of a building," Dave answered.

"What were the conditions, was it dry or wet?"

"When we found it, it was dry, but it had been rained on," Dave answered.

"Sarin is very potent, but over time, it will dissipate in water. If it was in the rain for a while, it was probably only about twenty percent effective. There's not enough on it now to be harmful," the tech added.

"Can you sterilize that piece of plastic to render it completely safe?" Dave asked.

"Yes sir, I can."

"Wait . . . is Sarin chemically marked to be able to determine origin?" Dave asked.

"No sir, but there were so few manufacturers that we have their formulas mapped and have built an in-house database."

"Where did this Sarin come from?"

The tech looked at the vertical lines like a submariner reading a sonar screen.

"Not from the US, the former USSR, Iraq, China, Syria, or any of the other seven countries we know that have stockpiled Sarin. I have no basis of comparison for this formula," the tech replied.

"Okay. Take what samples you need and sterilize the rest of the plastic for our analysis," Dave directed.

The tech spent the next thirty minutes cutting off a portion of the plastic and placing it in an airtight portable container that he would take back to his lab. He saturated the glass containment box with a fine mist of five percent bleach and ninety-five percent ionized water and used a small sprayer of the solution and soft brushes to scrub the plastic part. He rinsed it with distilled water and captured all of the liquids in sealed tanks onboard the truck.

Once satisfied the part was clean, he retested it.

"No residue left, sir," he reported.

He evacuated the now clean air through another filter, spun the black knobs, and opened the end of the glass case. Reaching in with a gloved hand, he retrieved the part. He used the portable Ion Mobility Spectrometer to sniff every inch of the plastic; the box did not emit a peep.

As if to show the quality of his work, the tech stripped off his gloves and presented the shiny black part to Dave with his bare hand. Dave nodded his approval and accepted the part.

The men folded their suits back into the travel cases, tied everything down in the back of the truck, and drove away.

Once back in the safe house, Dave passed the black plastic piece around to the three people he had begun to think of as his team and asked, "What is this part of?"

"It's part of whatever is in that covered antenna on the tower," Lydia suggested.

CHAPTER 45

The four of them raced back to the Wizard's command center, where the Wiz checked the accounts and announced that the frequency with which Battles was, or *thought* he was moving money had increased.

Battles had not figured out yet that even though his accounts showed fat balances, he actually didn't have possession of the money once he transferred it. The Wizard controlled the transferred money, and he was slowly bleeding it off to dozens of small accounts that Battles and his crew would never find.

Scotty had left one of his company trucks at the Wizard's for Dave to use. Dave's equipment was still in his truck at the Fairfax County Sheriff's impound lot. Dave had been receiving more and more urgent messages from Sheriff Dayton; he continued to ignore them. He would have some relationship building to do when this was over, but that would have to wait.

Battles and his band of thieves had gone eerily and mysteriously silent after the ambush attempt on Dave. Their lack of aggression could be explained by any number of possibilities: they may have felt Dave did not have any useful information, they believed he had lost the data on the USB drive in the house fire, or maybe they felt they had frightened Dave off with the fire and the ambush.

All of the scenarios posed a potentially lethal underestimation of Dave Walsh's abilities and determination. Dave loved nothing more than to be underestimated by his foes.

CHAPTER 46

"We are close, my brothers," Tarik spoke quietly to Ahmed and Hamza. He had called them together again in the library of the huge mansion for a final planning session.

Amina, quietly subdued, poured tea for them.

Tarik was the only one comfortable in the gentrified settings. Ahmed and Hamza were more comfortable on a mountaintop in Afghanistan wrapped in patoos and cradling AK-47s than they were sitting on five-thousand-dollar chairs.

"Prepare yourselves to travel in two days. We will take my airplane to the infidel's capital city. There, we will strike a mighty blow. We will put our plan in motion three days from now, on the day of Mawlid. The Prophet's day of birth will be the day we unleash our little birds of death. They will pour out of the sky and contaminate the water supply of thousands. Once we release the birds, we will also fly away to watch the chaos play out on the world's news networks."

Tarik did not tell his fellow Jihadists that over the past two months, he had been slowly and carefully short-selling millions of dollars of stock belonging to the largest US corporations.

He was also buying up millions of medical N95 masks and hundreds of ventilators to keep the lifesaving devices from the US at a time that they would be desperate for them.

He had a team of stockbrokers standing by to begin accelerated short-selling his stocks the day before the attack was scheduled. If his calculations were correct, he would reap billions of dollars from the coming stock market crash—a crash that he would initiate.

CHAPTER 47

"She's pretty savvy with computers," Jax whispered.

"And smart. We would have recruited her," Dave replied.

"What do you know about her?" Jax asked.

"Nothing other than what you've seen. She's got street smarts and she's tough."

"Do you mind if I have her checked out?" Jax asked.

"Looks like we don't have much of a choice at this point."

Lydia and the Wiz were in the command center, clicking furiously on various keyboards, trying to unravel the tower mystery. Dave and Jax were standing in the back, sipping coffee from white Styrofoam cups.

Jax walked out of the room to make a call. "They will check her out and call me back," he said when he returned.

"Show me how to project my computer screen onto the wall screen," Lydia asked Wiz.

He rolled his chair over, and with one hand, he showed her the keystrokes required.

She used Google Earth, zoomed in as close as possible, and captured a screenshot of the tower on the roof of the hospital. She placed the picture in a PowerPoint slide.

She then added red arrows to indicate the power generators and heavy electrical cables that would normally be
routed to the power-hungry antennas on the tower.

"Is there any doubt that this tower is a fake?" she
asked, looking around the room.

No disagreement from the three men staring at the
screen.

"We have to know what's in that covered antenna
dish," she said.

"Let me make a call," Jax said, as he picked up one
of the landlines in the command center. "Scotty, do you
still have some of those Black Hornets the Brits loaned
us in Kandahar?" Jax asked. He nodded his head as he
listened to Scott's answer. "Can you deploy one and push
data to an IP address we give you? You can? Great. We
need to get a look at a communication tower on the roof
of the Children's Medical Center near McMillan Reservoir. We need to keep this very low profile. Stand by for
Wiz."

Jax held the phone out to the Wizard and said,
"Give Scott an IP address that he can send a live video
feed to."

The Wizard gave Scott a string of eleven numbers
divided by three decimal points. Scott read the numbers
back to him and said he would send the video to that IP
address in a couple of hours. He also told the Wizard to
monitor Channel Bravo for voice comms. The Wizard
handed the phone back to Jax and began configuring his
communication gear to receive the video and audio feeds.

"Scotty, thanks. Talk to you soon."

"What was that about?" Lydia asked.

"The Brits have a very small remote-control helicopter Nano-drone. They call it the Black Hornet. It measures only one inch by four inches and weighs less than an ounce. They use the full-motion video to search areas just ahead of their troops for the enemy. It's almost impossible to hear in flight," said Jax.

For the next two hours, Wiz and Lydia dug deeper and deeper through cyberspace, trying to find the true owner of the tower.

CHAPTER 48

Scott arrived at the hospital and parked the undercover tactical van in the adjacent public parking lot. Today, the local cable company's metallic signs were affixed to its sides.

He spent fifteen minutes just sitting, looking around, and listening, trying to get a feel for the pulse of his surroundings.

One of the essential traits of a good operator is patience.

Once Scott understood what "normal" looked and sounded like in this environment, he felt it was safe to begin his operation.

He moved to the rear of the van and began opening desert-tan Storm Cases. The first one held the controller for the small helicopter drone. The second one opened to reveal a ten-inch by ten-inch monitor that would allow him to see in real time what the drone was seeing. The third, and smallest case, contained the Black Hornet Nano-drone. It fit easily into his hand completely assembled.

The freshly charged batteries would give him almost thirty minutes of flight and video.

He powered up the drone with a switch on its belly. A few keystrokes and the monitor blinked to life. A few more taps and an array of green lights indicated that he had good communication with the tiny drone.

Scott put on a lightweight headset, selected Channel B on the radio, and keyed the microphone.

"Dungeon, this is Gatsby, over."

The Wizard's command center call sign was obvious.

Scott's call sign was given to him by the teams because his name, Efron Scott, sounded like the author of *The Great Gatsby*.

"This is Dungeon," the Wiz answered.

"Comm check?" Scott asked.

"Lumpy Chicken," replied the Wiz, modifying the phonic alphabet for 'Loud and Clear.'

"Same here. Standing by for instructions," Scott indicated.

Scott heard Jax's voice over the headset. "We need a three-sixty flyby of the tower to start with. You will see a damaged antenna on one of the covered dishes. We need close-ups of that, if possible."

"Copy all. Ready to test video feed?"

"Roger. Send it," Wiz replied.

Scott tapped his keyboard and the camera in the nose of the Black Hornet came to life. The tiny rotor blades spun up to operating RPM as he held it in his hand. He checked to make sure he was transmitting to the correct IP address Wiz had given him earlier. It looked solid on his end.

"Good video, cleared to launch," Wiz told him, as he hit the record button on his console.

"Copy. Here we go."

With that, Scott opened the sliding door on the van, checked to see if anyone was looking his way, and pitched the tiny drone out. It immediately began to climb and head toward the tower on the roof of the hospital. Scott had programmed a GPS point and altitude near the tower into the drone's navigation system. He closed the door and took manual control of the drone. Using the video screen to orient himself, he flew the Black Hornet to within eight feet of the tower and commanded the drone to begin a slow upward spiral, keeping the camera of the small helicopter pointed at the tower.

"Solid video," Wiz relayed, as he began recording the video.

"Copy."

Once he had circled the tower several times, he began looking for the damaged antenna. It was a small tear and not readily visible, but he found it on his third pass. "Going in for a close-up of the damage," he transmitted.

"Copy. Good feed on this end," Wiz answered.

Scott hovered the small helicopter within inches of the tear in the cover of the dish. Calm winds helped him hold it steady while in close proximity to the steel structure.

"Gatsby, do you have a light on that thing?" Wiz asked.

"Stand by," Scott answered, as he toggled the command for a small, but very bright LED on the nose of the drone. "It's pretty hard on battery life so let me know when you're finished," he passed to the Wiz.

"Rog," Wiz acknowledged.

"Hold it right there!" the Wiz shouted into his mic.

The drone had illuminated some type of equipment housed in the covered antenna dish. It reflected light in a similar way to the shiny black plastic they'd found on the concrete.

"Unable. The winds are picking up; I can't hold it in that position," Scott radioed back.

"I've got to RTB, like now, or I won't get this thing back. It looks like a thunderstorm is heading this way."

"Rog. Terminate and recover. Thanks, Gatsby."

"No problem. I'll check in later. Gatsby out," Scott said, as he terminated the video link to the Dungeon.

"Play that back," Dave instructed the Wiz.

The Wizard rolled his chair to a rack and hit rewind on the DVD player. He backed the video up about three minutes and hit play. The big screen came back to life with the replay. Now he could pause it with his remote control.

The tear in the antenna dish was just a dark hole until the light from the drone was switched on.

The Wiz hit pause just as the light illuminated the contents. They could see what appeared to be a broken piece of black plastic like the one they'd found. They knew the implication of that; if the plastic piece they had found had Sarin on it and it came from the covered dish antenna, then the plastic in the covered antenna also contained Sarin.

"Let it play for a few seconds," Dave instructed.

Wiz hit play.

The video feed began to shake a little as the Nano drone was buffeted by the winds. The powerful, but narrow light beam swung further into the darkness of the antenna dish and flashed by more parts. "Stop there and rewind frame by frame," Dave said.

The Wiz did that and after about thirty frames, he paused.

They all saw it.

"Oh my God!" Lydia exclaimed, conveying what they were all thinking.

Small airplanes were nestled in the covered container where an antenna should have been. There appeared to be six of them fitted in the space.

"Roll the video back to the start," Dave once again directed.

The Wiz played the video from the beginning, and they all watched as the little Black Hornet flew toward the tower.

For a period of time, the entire screen was filled with only one terrestrial feature, the McMillan Reservoir, the source of water for most of Washington, DC.

CHAPTER 49

"What's the latest on Walsh?" Battles asked General Davis on a secure line.

"He's apparently gone to ground. We know he left the hospital after the ambush. His truck is still in the impound lot. My sources at the sheriff's office say the sheriff is upset that Walsh hasn't called him back. Maybe he's running," Davis replied.

"He's not running—he's planning something. I know this man. The only way he'll stop is if he's dead. He's relentless. Get your guys to find him. We have to contain him," Battles barked.

"I started moving the money. In another three days, all the accounts on that USB drive will be empty," Davis added.

"I saw the transfers," Battles said. "No one will be able to follow that trail."

"He could still get to us through the mineral rights contracts, although I'm not completely convinced that he ever opened the drive. Now that we don't have the girl any longer, he may back down," the general offered.

"We burned his house down and killed his housekeeper; do you really think he'll just let that go?" Battles asked sarcastically. "You better be preparing for war with this guy. He's coming."

"We can handle him," Davis replied, using skills he learned in the military establishment to sound sure of something he was not sure of at all.

"You better be able to," Battles said, and jabbed a button to disconnect the call.

CHAPTER 50

"We are going to have to take this to The Man," Jackson said to Dave, referring to the Director of National Intelligence, or DNI. He was the nation's top intelligence executive who reported daily to the president.

"What if he's part of Battles's group?" asked Dave.

"He's not. I know it. I know this man and he's not part of that," answered Jax.

"I thought I knew Battles too. I worked for him for the last five years. I thought I could trust him, but all of this makes me wonder about some of the assignments he gave me. Do *you* think Battles is part of the Sarin operation?" Dave asked.

"The guy is a liar, a thief, and a sociopath, but I can't believe that he's involved in this. I think he was used as a patsy to get the ground leases and expedite the construction," Jax offered, turning to address Lydia and the Wizard. "We need every data pack available on Battles."

CHAPTER 51

The Wizard and Lydia spent the next several hours searching for information on Warren Battles.

Lydia used the Internet for open source information; the Wizard used the classified systems that were available to him, hacking into the ones that weren't.

To Lydia, this was a lot like finding dirt on an asshole boyfriend.

To the Wiz, this was the first time he had ever turned his hacking skills on the people he worked for.

The techniques were the same . . . it just felt weird hacking into US military, Department of State, and intelligence community databases.

Dave and Jackson kept the pair fueled with pizza and Rockstar. Neither Wiz nor Lydia weighed more than a buck twenty, but they ate like every keystroke burned a thousand calories.

Suddenly, Wiz held his right index finger in the air as if bidding at a Christie's auction.

"I've got something!" he said. "I'm in Battles's administrative assistant's computer. I've not been able to hit his personal computer—yet."

"What can we get from that?" asked Jax.

"Let's see . . . I've got his appointment lists for the past six months, his 'to-do' list that his administrative assistant puts together for him, and his travel plans."

"Start with his 'to-do' and appointment lists and then give us his travel plans," Dave instructed.

"Okay, it looks like he has a meeting with the DNI tomorrow, and then a luncheon with the Sec-Def on Sunday."

"That's weird. Those guys don't usually meet on the weekends," Jax interrupted.

Wiz continued, "Then he's interviewing someone for an intern position on Monday, and he has lunch—

"Hold it! Did you say interviewing for an intern on Monday?" Dave asked.

"Yes, at ten a.m. Why?"

"Male or female?"

"Stand by." Wiz tapped keys and said, "Female. Here's her file: Samantha Tyler, age twenty-five. Selected from thirty applicants. The recruiter's notes show this will be her first face-to-face with anyone in the office."

"Is her picture in the file?" Dave asked.

"It's not in the employment file. Why?" Wiz inquired.

"We need to know more about Battles as quickly as possible, right?" Dave confirmed.

Heads nodded. "Then we need to get a bug in his office," he announced, as if this step was completely obvious.

The Wiz discreetly made eye contact with Jax, who had a half-smile on his face as his friend, Dave, nonchalantly planned the commission of a federal offense.

"Which female operative did you have in mind for this?" Jax asked.

"I'll do it!" Lydia volunteered quickly, and just as quickly wished she hadn't.

"No." Dave cut in. "You have no training for this type of operation. Absolutely not," he added emphatically.

"Well, she does look a little bit like her," Wiz offered weakly, while looking at Samantha Tyler's Facebook page.

"Wait . . ." Jax said. "We don't know how much time we have before something happens with that tower, but the clock's running. The interview is two days from now. I doubt we could get an undercover operative up to speed that quickly, not to mention the time it would take to secure a Presidential Finding or a search warrant. Lydia has shown good instincts; this is no different than the field expedient solutions we used when we were in the sandbox."

"No!" Dave said, raising his voice. "Sarah's not right for this. I won't allow it."

The men in the room froze at Dave's use of his deceased daughter's name. Dave didn't realize what he'd said.

"What?" he asked. "Why are you looking at me like that?"

"You said, 'Sarah's not right for this.' We're talking about Lydia, Dave," Jax gently reminded his friend.

Dave momentarily closed his eyes, his face set in pain. Without making eye contact, he walked out of the command center.

Jax followed Dave into the kitchen as the Wiz told Lydia about Sarah. Dave looked at Jax as he entered and held his hand up, palm out.

"I won't let anything happen to that girl, Jax," he said.

"I agree, and we won't. We will only be minutes from her. It's in a public setting. She has lots of street smarts and good intuition: she'll know if she needs to bail. Look, we can put a wire on her if you want, but we're sitting on a time-bomb. This is no longer about bank accounts or mineral rights—it's about a possible terrorist attack against our country. We've got to get more information immediately on who paid Battles to secure those tower sites," Jax said.

Dave hung his head.

The Wiz and Lydia spent the rest of Saturday night sifting through all the data they could find on Battles and the tower owners with very little success. The bugging operation seemed the best, close-in opportunity.

The Wiz began a background search on Samantha Tyler. Having had no previous government service, her information was not protected by high-level security measures, making her an easy target. It always amazed the Wiz how much personal information people published online. He was certain a lot of spies were out of a job because of that. It didn't take spy skills to data mine someone's background if they gave it to you for free on countless social media sites.

Samantha Tyler was no different than her contemporaries in terms of publishing everything about herself—and her whereabouts—every waking hour. In a very short period of time, the Wiz had a complete dossier on her, including birth date, cell phone number, address, names and addresses of her roommates, parents and siblings, every school she had attended, and details about both her ex-boyfriends and her current boyfriend.

He had pictures of every trip she had ever taken and the names of her favorite musicians and foods. He knew her clothing style and which gym she belonged to. He checked Uber and knew the places she frequented. He could see the restaurants she liked and that she could write a fairly decent critique on Yelp. He knew which movies she had rented and what she posted about them. He knew what political party she supported and what type of car she drove.

All of this came from the Internet; he hadn't even touched the DMV, the court system, her banking information, or her previous employers' databases.

Within hours, the Wiz could have completely taken over Samantha Tyler's identity. He knew more about her than she knew about herself. He definitely knew much more about her than would be necessary for a thirty-minute interview for an intern position; however, they were sending a rookie into the top intelligence agency in the world.

Overpreparation was warranted in this situation.

Once the Wiz had compiled the data, they all met with Lydia in one of the small conference rooms.

"Are you sure you want to do this?" Jax asked Lydia.

"Yes. I've had time to think about it, and yes, I think I can pull this off," she said, making eye contact with each man.

"Okay. We'll be in the building as back-up. You will be wearing a transmitting device.

We've been in these offices dozens of times. They don't have active RF detectors so they won't be able to intercept signals from your transmitter. We'll also give you a small microphone to leave behind in Battles's office," Jax briefed.

"Okay," Lydia nodded, afraid that if she said any more, she might reveal the enormous fear she felt at volunteering for such a task.

"Good. Wiz, give her the lowdown on Samantha Tyler."

For the next couple of hours, the Wiz showed Lydia numerous personal photos, webpages, and bank statements, as well as pictures of Tyler's car and apartment. As Samantha had laid her life out for all the world to see, the Wiz was able to brief Lydia on every aspect of Samantha Tyler's existence.

Lydia nodded and took it all in; she had an excellent capacity for remembering details.

At the end of the briefing, Wiz began questioning Lydia about Samantha. As she answered the broad questions correctly, he began asking more and more esoteric questions. She nailed those also.

"Lydia!" Dave called from behind her. She didn't turn in response.

"Samantha," he called, and she turned with a smile.

"Was that a test?" she asked.

"It wasn't intended to be, but if it had been, you would've passed," he said.

CHAPTER 52

Ahmed had been on a lot of airplanes, all Russian-built. His flights to Damascus, Baghdad, Sana'a, and Kabul, in support of Jihad were always crowded and smelled of hydraulic oil and body sweat.

Ahmed had never seen opulence like this.

Surely this was not in keeping with the Prophet's teachings.

He was speechless as he climbed the airstairs and sat in the seat Tarik pointed to. The cream-colored leather seat had gold seatbelt buckles. There were several large screen monitors on the walls of the jet. Toward the rear of the airplane, he saw a large desk stacked with communication gear. Hamza sat across the aisle from him. Ahmed hoped he did not look as wide-eyed as Hamza.

Tarik, sitting at the big desk, picked up the phone and spoke sharply into it.

He moved from his desk to a seat across from Ahmed as the co-pilot pushed a button to retract the airstairs. The huge Gulfstream 550 began to taxi for take-off.

As the aircraft climbed, Ahmed thought about what Tarik had told them. *They were going to America to "stab the beast in the heart."*

Ahmed was a devoted warrior. He would do as he was told.

He knew the attack had to do with the Sarin they had stolen and the little airplanes the scientists had put the poison into, but he had been given no information about his role.

Once the jet leveled off, Tarik moved back to the desk and had the two men join him in the seats facing him.

"I will give you your orders now," he said, as he opened a large manila envelope and began removing documents.

He handed each man a new passport with counterfeit US visas identifying them as Jordanians. Tarik then removed aerial photographs depicting the towers adjacent to the reservoirs and street maps of the areas surrounding the tower sites. An hour of detailed site briefings ensued as he moved to the operational phase of the plan.

He placed three electronic controllers the size of a deck of playing cards, on his desk. Each controller had two square buttons on its face.

"This is how you will initiate the attack. You will turn it on here," he demonstrated, sliding a switch on the side of the controller. One of the buttons on the controller began blinking red. "You will push the blinking button. When you do, you will hear three small explosions as the covers on the antennas blow off," he said, pointing to the drum-shaped antennas on the photograph.

"You will then need to wait four minutes for the navigation system of the little birds to initialize. Once the system is stable, this other button"—he indicated on the front of the controller——¬"will begin blinking green. When it blinks, push it.

"That will free the UAVs to fly. They will start dropping out of the antenna dish and begin their programmed flights over the reservoir. Their program will then command them to dive into the water, releasing the poison. Once you see the little birds begin to fly, go to your next tower and do the same. When you have successfully executed your mission, return to the airport. We will get back on this airplane and leave the country.

"Any questions?" Tarik asked, looking at each man.

Hamza avoided eye contact, but Ahmed spoke up. "What if we are challenged either on the way to the tower, or as we trigger the device?" he asked.

"I will have weapons for you when we land. You are not to let anything or anyone prevent you from executing your mission, understand?" Tarik answered.

"Yes," Ahmed replied.

"We will now go over the maps. Since you are not familiar with driving in America, I have drivers assigned to each of you. Once they return you safely back to the airport, they will be happy to give their lives for Jihad."

He looked both men in the eye to be sure they understood. They both gave a slight nod.

Once finished with the attack plans, he instructed the men to return to their seats and get some rest.

Tarik used the plane's satellite link to check his bank accounts. Short-selling of his stocks had consumed a lot of his financial reserves, resulting in a significant dip in his cash accounts. Some of the shorts were bought on a margin, borrowing money to cover the shorts. He alone knew the market rise he was betting against would never happen.

If ever there was a sure thing in the market, this was it.

Major stocks were going to tank, especially the insurance companies he had heavily shorted.

His attacks would be the reason for their demise, and the key to his increased fortune.

CHAPTER 53

Attempting to run every possible scenario through his mind and knowing that missing even one of the hundreds of meticulous details required for a successful operation could endanger his team gave Dave a restless night.

The team had one full day to get ready for the interdiction op against Battles, and everyone was up early. Jax ran out and retrieved coffee and bagels from a nearby Panera.

"Scotty's on the way with the equipment," Jax announced as the others gathered in the kitchen.

"We need to take Lydia shopping for clothes. I've downloaded some photos of Samantha and know what she would probably wear for the interview," Wiz began, out of the blue. He opened his laptop and began paging through pictures of Samantha. They showed her in a white starched shirt, blue blazer, and a very short, navy-blue pencil skirt.

"So, I did a little research, and we need to get Lydia a Croft & Barrow slim-fit dress shirt in white, a J. Crew No.2 pencil skirt in navy blue, an H&M navy blue blazer, Talera pumps by Earthies in navy blue, and a Kate Spade New York Metro watch."

Everyone was afraid to speak. Suddenly, they all started laughing.

"What?" the Wiz said.

"Um, that's very specific," Jax said, as the others tried to stifle their laughter.

"Yes, it is. I just researched the look she was wearing and found those items. She can get everything at the mall, which is open today," he added, still not understanding the group's amazement. "Oh, and she'll need a haircut and some makeup," he added to their now unbridled laughter.

Dave, Jax, and Lydia spent almost five hours at the mall; despite his objections, Wiz was directed to stay at the Dungeon to continue researching the antennas.

Lydia went shopping and had her hair styled, while Dave and Jax sat on the benches in the mall, providing loose security. This shopping trip cost considerably more than the stop at Goodwill.

When they returned to the Dungeon, Scott was there with the electronic hardware. "I like what you've done to your hair," Scott said to Lydia.

She shot him a one-finger wave as she walked past.

"I meant it . . ." he said defensively.

"She's a little bit touchy," offered Wiz.

Scott placed a black Storm Case in the middle of the kitchen table and opened it.

Everyone gathered around.

"This is the body wire you will wear," he said as he handed Lydia a necklace. It looked like it was made of gold and had small coins on it. "One of the coins is a microphone and one is a battery. The battery is good for about four hours." Next, he handed her a bracelet with several small stones that looked like turquoise and one dull brown larger stone dangling from it.

"This bracelet has the part you will leave behind. The larger brown stone is a transmitter. You'll pull that stone off your bracelet and drop it in the planter in his private office. It looks like the other rocks he has in his planters. You don't have to activate it. The transmitter will be on from the time we give it to you. It will transmit for about a week before the battery runs down."

Lydia nodded her understanding; she didn't have any questions and was as prepared as she was going to be. Now, she just wanted to get it over with.

Jax ordered Chinese food; Scott went to pick it up. With everyone absorbed in their own thoughts about the next day's unknowns, the atmosphere in the safehouse was unusually subdued as they ate.

CHAPTER 54

When Lydia walked into the kitchen on Monday morning in her Samantha Tyler disguise, all three guys instantly stopped their small talk. She looked stunning in her professional business attire and new hairstyle.

"What?" she said, looking around at the guys.

"You look amazing," Jax said, stating the obvious.

"Oh, these old rags?" She smiled playfully and did a slow turn for them.

"Holy shit," was all the Wiz could utter. "Don't worry about the interview—your mental abilities will be the last thing he will be considering," the Wiz offered.

Jax drove Dave and Lydia to the heart of DC.

The ride was quiet; there was no last-minute coaching or rehearsing. If Lydia didn't know her role by now, it was too late. Dave turned to her from the front passenger seat just as she opened the rear door to step out.

"You'll do great, and we'll be ready to come and get you if it goes south," he said.

"I'll be fine," Lydia said with more conviction than she felt.

She could feel her underarms begin to perspire as she approached the office building. Feeling nauseous, she pulled open the heavy, bulletproof doors and approached the security checkpoint. When asked for ID, she presented the security guard with a Virginia driver's license bearing her own photo, but Samantha Tyler's name.

It was her first real test.

She looked up at the security cameras and wondered who was watching her. Did she look as scared as she felt? The security guard handed her license back to her. Lydia didn't realize she'd been holding her breath.

The Wiz's prowess with fake IDs had guaranteed her overcoming the guard's scrutiny.

"I'm here for an interview with Mr. Battles," she said.

The guard handed her a lanyard and laminated badge with a bold red "V" printed on it, which she hung around her neck. Another security guard emerged from his office and motioned her to follow him toward the elevators. He opened the door with his card key and selected the floor for her.

"The elevator will stop on the Deputy Director's floor. You will see his office suite when you step off," he said.

The real Samantha Tyler was at home after receiving a call that the interview had been postponed one week. One of Scott's men was watching her apartment and car to make sure she stayed there. The Wiz was also monitoring her phones from the comm center to make sure she didn't try to call Battles's office. He had reprogrammed the routing so that if she did call, it would ring Wiz's phone.

Dave and Jax entered the building through a service entrance using an ID swipe card the Wiz had provided them. They went to a floor that was under construction just below the DDNI's office. Their monitors worked perfectly, and they could hear everything Lydia was saying. So far, so good.

At first, Lydia sounded a little nervous, but the further she got into her role, the stronger she became.

Finally—the moment of truth.

She stopped outside of the office suite of the DDNI, and before entering, unbuttoned one more of her shirt's top buttons. Satisfied, she entered Battles's offices and presented herself to the receptionist.

"Hi, I'm Samantha Tyler. I'm here for an intern interview at ten a.m.," she said, in a strong, confident voice.

"Hi, Samantha. Welcome! I'm Tiffany. We have you on Mr. Battles's schedule. The staff will want to talk to you for a few minutes first. Then we will take you to meet Deputy Director Battles. May I offer you some tea, coffee, or water?" Tiffany asked.

"Water would be fine," Lydia replied.

"Okay. I'll get that for you. If you'll just have a seat over there, we'll be right with you," Tiffany said with a practiced smile.

The questions from the staff were all softballs—no real meat on them.

"Where have you worked before? What do your parents do? Can you work long hours? How far do you live from here? Do you have your own car? Are you willing to be submitted for a top secret clearance investigation? Will you submit to a polygraph?"

She must have given all the correct answers because at the end, Chase—apparently the lead staffer—said, "We will go in to visit Deputy Director Battles in just a minute. Address him as Mr. Battles. Look him in the eye when you answer questions and tell the truth."

Then he smiled the professional smile they all seemed to employ.

Chase opened a dark walnut door and ushered Lydia into a massive office.

He closed the door behind him, leaving her alone with Battles.

Battles was on the phone and didn't look up as Lydia entered. He continued issuing directives over the phone and then disconnected. He looked up as if he didn't know anyone was in his office.

"Oh, hi!" he said, as he stood up and offered his hand.

Lydia took it and gave him a firm handshake. His eyes went directly to her chest. When he raised them to meet hers, her fear spiked and she fought to overcome her flight instincts. His eyes were dark and predatory; she felt he could see her deception. Her fear threatening to blot out her real assignment, all she wanted to do was to turn and run.

"So, you want to be an intern at the ODNI?" he asked.

"Yes sir," she answered meekly, her bravado abandoning her for a moment. "I want a career in the intelligence community. I have a degree in political science and think the DNI is the pinnacle of our intelligence efforts." Lydia's coached replies bolstered her and gave her courage.

"The intelligence business requires long hours. Are you willing to put in the time it will take to learn this business?" he asked.

"Yes, sir. I am very focused and determined. I know I can learn what will be required to contribute to your mission."

Just then his phone rang. "Excuse me while I take this," Battles said, as he answered the phone. Battles swiveled his chair away from her and continued his conversation in a hushed voice. Lydia took the opportunity to walk around his office as if impressed at being in the presence of power and position. She pretended to read the titles of the books arranged on a large bookcase.

With her back to him, she pulled the brown stone from her bracelet, palmed it, and discreetly dropped it in the planter that contained a six-foot ficus tree, shielding the action with her body. She looked closely and could not tell her stone from the rocks already in the planter, all the while better appreciating the fact that Dave and Jax had spent time in this office and were familiar with the layout and furnishings.

Battles hung up the phone and exchanged a few more pleasantries with the girl he had already decided would be his next intern and future conquest before calling Chase back in and dismissing her.

Battles asked Chase to remain for a minute as Lydia left his office.

Chase instructed Lydia to wait for him in the outer office.

When Chase came out of Battles's office, he said, "We will be in touch with you in the next few days. You made quite an impression on him."

Tiffany led her out of the office and said, "It was a pleasure meeting you. I hope to see you in the future."

"Thank you, it was a pleasure meeting you too," Lydia said, thinking she never wanted to see Tiffany or this office again.

Tiffany scanned her badge and selected the destination floor for Lydia as the security guard had done earlier. Once the elevator doors closed, her anxiety spiked. She was almost out . . . another few minutes and she would be away from here. She began to breathe as Dave had shown her on that first day. He called it combat breathing: breathe in for four seconds, hold for four seconds, breathe out for four seconds, hold for four seconds.

Her nerves calmed now, Lydia turned in her visitor's ID, retrieved her driver's license, and pushed through the heavy glass doors to the outside. The air felt wonderful as it cooled the sweat under the arms of her new blouse. She felt like she had just escaped death.

Within seconds, Jax's truck pulled to the curb and she climbed into the back seat. They drove away, headed to the Wizard's.

Dave looked at Lydia. She looked terrified, which was normal for an "operator's" first mission. "You were perfect," Dave praised from the front seat. "We heard it all. The Wiz reported good comms with the bug. How do you feel?"

"Guys, I've really got to pee," was all Lydia could manage.

Dave and Jax laughed at her unintentional comic relief.

CHAPTER 55

"The bug is working. I have good signal strength and clarity," the Wiz announced when they returned to the Dungeon.

"What was it like?" Wiz asked Lydia.

"I don't think he saw me plant the bug, but it felt like he could see right through me. I had the feeling he knew I wasn't who I said I was."

"I don't think he was looking *through* you," the Wiz said, looking at her unbuttoned shirt.

She looked down, looked up at the Wiz, and refastened one of the top buttons.

Once she finished giving the details and answering Dave and Jax's questions, Lydia went to the bathroom to change out of her Samantha disguise.

Dave and Jax pulled up chairs beside the Wiz's computer. Wiz said, "I've got a program running that is not only recording Battles, but it is also transcribing everything he's saying. I haven't been able to penetrate his phone lines yet. They are protected with trip-wires, which will trigger an alarm if I try to break in. The alarm will initiate security protocols that would likely include an RF sweep of his office, and that would hit on our bug. It wouldn't take them long to figure out who put it there since Lydia is on their security cameras. So, for now, we will have to settle for only one side of his conversations."

CHAPTER 56

"Mr. Battles, here are the latest stock market analysts' reports," one of his assistants said.

She laid the papers on Battles's desk and quickly left the office. Battles couldn't keep up with their names any longer. It seemed like an endless stream of young people cycled through his office.

Now, that young intern he interviewed earlier in the day had promise. Battles liked the way she looked him in the eye, and he liked the way she looked overall. He would have to try to work that—he hadn't tapped one that young in a while. She looked like she would be quite energetic in bed. Thoughts of her distracted him as he reviewed the recent market trends.

He almost missed it.

There was some serious market shorting going on. Most of the major insurance companies were being shorted. The last time that happened was just prior to 9/11. Aggressive short-selling of insurance company stock meant someone was betting that their stock would tank once they began paying out huge loss claims. If, in fact, the stock dropped dramatically in price, stock speculators stood to make a fortune.

"Chase! Get in here!" Battles yelled across the office.

"Yes sir?" Chase answered seconds later, standing tall in front of Battles's desk.

"Did you review these stock market reports?"

"Yes, sir, I did," he reported.

"Did you notice the short sales?"

"Yes, sir, I did."

"Find out who is shorting the market. I want that information within the hour."

"I'm on it, sir," Chase said as he pivoted and raced to his phone. In fifty-eight minutes, he was back in front of Battles's desk, presenting the report, like an offering, to his boss.

"Sir, it looks like a conglomerate from Austria is the main group buying the shorts. They are shorting not only insurance companies, but transportation, airlines, some public utilities, and even health care. The company's name and the principal's name are in that report."

"That will be all," Battles said, as he dismissed his minion.

He had begun reading and dissecting the report when he stopped cold.

Austria. That's odd. They're not exactly known for their risk-taking in international stock markets.

Tarik Basik? Holy shit! That's my guy. How did Basik go from selling mineral rights and communication towers to big time stock market speculation?

Battles closed the file and folded his hands on top of it while he pondered this.

That little fuck knows of an attack coming against the US! If an attack occurs, and the analysts are correct, Tarik stands to make billions of dollars.

Battles knew buying short required exquisite timing.

If the stock was bought too soon and it went up instead of down, the losses could be astronomical. The stock usually had to fall within a few days to make the risk pay off.

He knew the right thing to do was to notify the DNI and tell him an attack was imminent. Battles chose the opposite of the right thing to do: he called Tarik. Tarik answered on the second ring.

"Mr. Marshall, how are you?" Battles cooed, using Tarik's code name.

"Fine, sir, and you?" Tarik played along.

Battles got right to the point. "I understand you've been busy shorting the market."

Cold fear slashed at Tarik.

How could he know this? This could change everything I've planned—not the attack necessarily, but certainly the financial payoff. Battles could make some calls and suspend the market. This would effectively cancel all my trades, leaving me in debt for hundreds of millions of dollars.

"That's interesting information," Tarik replied, trying to hold his voice steady.

"Are you in the US?" Battles asked.

"Yes, I am."

"Meet me at the Greek restaurant in one hour."

"I will see you there," Tarik replied, and disconnected.

CHAPTER 57

There was no time for his usual thirty-minute recon of the restaurant. Tarik positioned Ahmed across the street to watch the front door and Hamza in the alley to watch the back.

He briefly considered killing Battles and pressing on with the attack. He decided to hold back unless Battles knew about the attack, and planned to prevent it. But knowing Warren Battles as well as he did, he was certain that Battles was going to be looking to him for a payday.

"Mr. Marshall, how nice of you to work me into your schedule," Battles said with more than a little bit of sarcasm.

"It is my pleasure," Tarik offered, poker-faced.

Battles wasted no time in getting down to business. "I know you're up to something. Slowly but steadily, you've been shorting the markets. We analyze the markets for just that type of activity; it's usually a precursor to an attack on our country."

Tarik knew this was the tipping point.

Either Battles turns me in to the authorities, or I demand money to stay silent.

Tarik's thumb surreptitiously hovered over the "Send" button on his phone. If he punched it, Ahmed and Hamza would come in, guns blazing, and pull Tarik out. They would have to hide from a massive manhunt until they could release the UAVs, and then race to the airport, leaving this country in ruin.

Battles leaned in and lowered his voice. "Our analysts say you stand to make ten billion dollars if the market falls to the level you anticipate. The only way that could happen would be if you knew of a plot to attack the US. So, listen carefully: I don't want to know your plan; I want a cut. I want half. Five billion paid to my account."

Tarik could not believe what he was hearing.

This high-level intelligence operative has just sold out his country. Five billion? That isn't even a rounding error on the billions I will make. I will agree to the five billion, and then I will kill this worthless bastard before I ever pay him a cent.

Tarik pretended to stammer and pause as he reluctantly agreed to Battles's demands. He stood up and left the restaurant. He had a lot to do to get ready for tomorrow's glorious event.

Efron Scott, in a navy, pin-striped suit he only wore to investors meetings, sat three tables away covertly photographing Tarik and Battles as they sat together in the Greek restaurant. He recorded their entire conversation using a miniature laser microphone.

The bug in Battles's office had tipped the Wiz off about the meeting.

Three of Scott's men were outside, taking photos and videos of Tarik and two tough-looking men as they gathered back at Tarik's SUV. The last shots they took were of his license plate as he drove away.

CHAPTER 58

Dave and Jax analyzed the photos and recordings that Scott brought to the Dungeon.

After listening to the audio twice, Dave said, "An attack is imminent and that fuck, Battles, is cognizant and not doing anything to stop it. Who are those three guys, Scott?" he asked as he looked at the surveillance photos from both inside and outside the restaurant.

"We're working on that now. We have two of the three names. The guy who met Battles rented the SUV under the name Jonathan Marshall. That's probably a cover. The Wiz says Battles's appointment book shows that he has met with him before, with the last time being about four months ago, just before the tower construction on the hospital began. We're still digging, but we feel like he is the owner of the other two towers as well. We may need to bring in Homeland Security on this."

"We can't," Jax pointed out. "One call to them, and their next phone call will be to Battles. We have to work this one ourselves. Hell, I can't even energize my office on this for the same reason."

"We got a solid hit on one of Marshall's security guys who was stationed outside the restaurant. His name is Ahmed Azzi, a Kosovar. We have him showing up in a lot of bad places just before bad shit happens," Scott said.

"Dave! Dave! You're going to want to hear this!" the Wizard yelled from his console.

Dave, Jax, and Scott walked into the darkened room where the Wiz had the audio from Battle's office on speaker. It quickly became clear that Battles was speaking to the DNI.

"Yes, Mr. Director, I'm sure of it: Walsh has been associating with an Austrian banker by the name of Tarik Basik. We intercepted a phone call between Tarik and Walsh discussing some kind of action against the United States."

"No sir, I am not sure when it is going to happen. Our analysts think it could be in the next few weeks. Yes sir, I'm sure."

"My recommendation? I recommend we pick up Walsh for questioning. We need to find out what he knows and begin a forensic analysis of his banking records."

"No sir, we do not have time for a warrant. We need to bring him in under the Patriot Act and sweat him for information."

"Sir, we know Walsh has a lot of goodwill on the Hill. To make sure we were not on a witch hunt, we conducted a cursory search of Walsh's finances. We found an account in the Bahamas, in his name, containing one million dollars."

"No sir, it was not inherited and it does not match the insurance payout when his wife and daughter were killed. He has been a government employee his entire career. The deposit is recent."

"Yes sir, we will use the utmost discretion."

"Yes sir, I will keep you posted."

With that, Battles disconnected and could be heard punching in another phone number.

"Mike, I want your guys to find Dave Walsh. The DNI has authorized me to pick him up for questioning. No, I'm not going to get my team to do it. I need to keep this off the books. Mike, he needs to die in a shoot-out. Yes, that's right. Make it happen." Battles disconnected the call.

Dave and his team next heard Battles laughing like an insane man.

Jax watched Dave closely during the audio session: he knew his friend well. He saw the vein on Dave's temple begin to throb as he set his jaw.

"Dave," he said. No response. "Dave!"

Walsh turned.

Jax saw the killer instinct in his friend's face.

"Dave, we have to finesse this. This is not the time for direct action. Dave! Are you listening?" Jax tried to reach him.

Turning immediately to the Wiz, Jax ordered, "Find that account in the Bahamas. I want to know who set it up and when. Make a copy of that recording we just heard and find out who this Tarik Basik is. We're going to see the DNI, now, before Battles gets this information on the street.

"Dave, we have a plan. We are going to handle this with discretion. You can't storm the castle—that's exactly what Battles wants. If you do, then you will be exactly who he is portraying you to be. Don't you see?" Jax pleaded.

Before Dave could respond, Wiz said, "Holy shit! Look!" He had pulled Tarik Basik's data and had his picture on the big screen. Tarik was none other than Jonathan Marshall, the guy who had met Battles in the Greek restaurant. It took a moment, but they all came to the same conclusion: Battles was going to wait until after the attack to name Tarik Basik as the terrorist. By that time, Battles would already have his money and Basik would be on the run.

Battles would profit from his country's misery and suffering while being hailed as a hero for outing the terrorist. Furthermore, implicating Dave in the terrorist activity would deflect attention away from Battles and solve his "Dave Walsh" problem.

"Okay, get me every electron this Basik guy has ever generated. We need it right now. I'm pretty sure the fuse has been lit on this attack, and we have to get out in front of it," Jax ordered.

"Dave, Scotty, a minute?" Jax asked, as he walked into the kitchen. "Here's the beginning of a plan. It may not be *the* plan, but it's *a* plan. Shoot holes in it as you see necessary," Jax began. "First, we take the information we just got from Battles to the DNI. Battles is not going public with this because he wants you dead, not in custody. So, we have some time.

"Second, I think we all agree that these three towers are tied to whatever plot these assholes are planning. At least one of them has Sarin-impregnated UAVs stored in the fake satellite dish; so, we have to assume the other two contain Sarin also.

"From the permits, we know the locations of the other two towers. We have to secure all three towers and disable the UAVs without allowing them into the atmosphere. Scotty, we're going to need three six-man teams, one team for each tower."

"Roger that. I can get the manpower, but what do we do once we get to the towers?" Scott asked.

"I don't know just yet," Jax answered.

"Fire," Dave said. "We use fire. Fire destroys the Sarin, but it has to be persistent. The fire has to destroy all the drones before they take flight. We need something like Napalm."

"Can you get your team to meet us at the Schoolhouse at 0800 hours tomorrow?" Jax asked.

"We'll be there," Scott said as he headed for the door.

"Let's go visit the DNI," Jax said to Dave.

CHAPTER 59

Jackson Baer had no problem getting an emergency meeting with the Director of National Intelligence. He just "forgot" to mention that Dave Walsh was going to be with him.

Jax and Dave both greeted the director's administrative assistant, Mona Solano, as they passed her desk and entered his office.

The DNI flinched when Dave followed Jax into his office. He picked up the phone to call security, but Jax held up his hand. "Mr. Director, wait one second."

They began placing evidence of the tower plot on the DNI's desk.

Five minutes into the briefing, the DNI pushed back from his desk and said, "I get it. How many towers and where are we on the timeline for the attack?"

"We have solid evidence that the fake antennas on the hospital tower contain the drones and Sarin. We suspect the other two towers do as well. We don't know the timeline, but we believe it's soon," replied Jax. "On the way over, I received a call from the chem warfare analyst, giving me a rundown on the piece of plastic we found on the hospital roof.

"At one time, the porous surface of the plastic had a foam backing along with a unique membrane making it airtight and sealing in the Sarin. But the membrane melts when it comes in contact with water; the foam, covered by the plastic, is soaked with Sarin. When the plastic and foam combination is dropped into water, the Sarin is released, contaminating the water immediately.

"We feel they intend to fly the small UAVs, shown in the photos, into DC's water sources. We need a hazmat team to contain the UAVs and dismantle the antenna dishes before they are launched from the towers," Jax concluded.

"Earlier today, I received a call from Battles implicating you, Dave," stated the DNI. "Tell me why that is not the case."

Dave and Jax looked at each other before speaking.

Jax offered, "We have evidence that Battles helped Tarik Basik, an Albanian working as a banker in Austria, expedite the permitting for three towers, including the one on the hospital.

At that point, we felt he was unwitting in terms of the Sarin plot. Subsequently, Battles discovered the stock market was being shorted by Basik. Battles met with him and asked for a cut of his potential gains."

"And you know this how?" the DNI asked.

Dave stepped in. "We bugged Battles's office and then surveilled his meet with Basik."

"Let me get this straight: you placed an illegal listening device in my Deputy DNI's office?"

"Yes, sir. Time was short. We have other information on him, as well," Dave replied, and then he went on to explain how the whole operation was unraveled because of a stolen USB drive.

The DNI was stunned when he heard the names of the co-conspirators. When he found his voice, he said, "Oh my God. I've got to take this to the president. It will likely mean my job. The public backlash may push him out of office as well. I'll deal with that later. Right now, we must stop this attack.

"Homeland Security has a hazmat team based at the airport. They practice this type of scenario every month. Let's get them rolling. We can augment with local law enforcement, US military, or National Guard forces as we need to," the director confirmed.

"Sir, we may want to reconsider that. If we go with the 'Big Boys,' the press will be on this instantly. What if you handle the hospital tower with the Homeland guys, but let us handle the other two towers? We have a small team meeting first thing in the morning. We can put together the resources to dismantle these antennas, making it look like part of a construction project," Jax offered.

The Director paused for a minute, thinking through that scenario.

"Get your guys rolling. You're right—it will cause mass panic if this goes public. If we move quickly enough, we may contain this before the attack can be triggered. I expect you to call me immediately if you need backup, and I'll send in the cavalry. Also, get this guy, Tarik Basik, into custody," the DNI ordered.

Dave and Jax left the DNI's office as he was yelling commands to his staff. "Mona! Get a security detail up here and call Deputy Battles to my office. Immediately!" he barked.

"Yes sir," she answered.

Mona called Warren Battles. He was in his office.

She whispered into the phone, "I don't know what's going on, but the DNI told me to call for a security detail and he wants you to come to his office. I think the security detail is for you. Dave Walsh and Jackson Baer were just here."

"Shit . . . tell him you haven't been able to find me."

"Okay," she said. Before she could add anything else, Battles disconnected the call.

CHAPTER 60

Homeland Security's CBRNE (chemical, biological, radioactive, nuclear & explosive) blue panel trucks, along with local police and fire units, began arriving at the Children's National Hospital.

A large Incident Command Center was established in the main parking lot. In addition, the hospital was surrounded and all streets were blocked off by local law enforcement. Helicopters began circling the hospital like angry bees; their job was to secure the area using FLIR and FMV to detect anyone trying to enter or escape the perimeter. With the help of first responders, hospital staff moved patients off of the upper floors.

Once his team was assembled in the parking lot, the lead hazmat technician began his briefing by pointing to the tower with the three drum-like antennas.

"The antenna dishes on the tower contain small UAVs that are soaked in Sarin. We need to secure the covers on those dishes, remove each dish—with its cover intact—from the tower, and place the entire assembly in an airtight bag," he said.

He then laid out a six-step plan.

CBRNE technicians dressed in hazmat suits trundled into the hospital and crossed the lobby to the elevators. The first firemen in the building keyed the elevators to fire department mode, sending the cars to the lobby. The doors automatically locked open until keyed again. Three suited techs entered and selected the top floor. They exited the elevator and shuffled toward the roof access door, waiting for additional techs and equipment to arrive. Once the team and equipment were in place on the roof, they would begin to execute the plan.

First, the bomb disposal team would check for anti-tamper explosives. If present, they would disarm them. Second, the hazmat team would use quick-drying construction adhesive to glue a heavy rubber patch to the outside of the antenna dish to cover the previously damaged area. Third, they would use a metal banding machine, like the type used to bundle lumber, to secure the cover to the dish of the antenna. Fourth, a portable crane would be assembled on the roof. Two high-angle rescue men would climb the tower and attach the crane's cable. They would unbolt the antenna, allowing the crane to lower it into a huge rubber bag. Fifth, a helicopter would sling-load the bag off the roof and into a waiting hazmat containment truck.

Finally, the deadly load would be transported to Dugway Proving Grounds to be analyzed and destroyed.

The determined crew would work through the night, pushing the darkness away with powerful floodlights. By morning, the tower on the roof of the Children's National Hospital would be neutered.

CHAPTER 61

Colin Pierce unstrapped his four-point harness and crawled out of the airplane.

The sound of the huge engines ticking as they cooled was the only noise on the dark airport ramp.

He leaned against the side of the aircraft, letting the soft spring night wash over him and begin drying the sweat-soaked flight suit that was sticking to his back. Fishing his cell phone out of his pocket, Colin saw that he had a missed call from Jackson Baer. It had been received a little over an hour ago. He highlighted the call and pushed send.

No preamble—they went straight into the requirement like when they were overseas in the "bad ole days."

"Hey. I need your help. What do the next couple of days look like for you?" Jax asked.

"I just finished a fourteen-hour day—seven of those chasing some dude from a drug bust, but I'll start driving now if you need me," Colin answered.

"No, not tonight, but tomorrow," Jax replied.

"Okay. When and where?"

"Briefing at the schoolhouse tomorrow at 0800 hours. We will need some ISR and top cover for an up-coming off-the-books op."

"I'm in, and I'll check with my boss for the airplane. He knows you from some previous work. I'm sure he'll support whatever you need."

And just like that, Colin had agreed to help an old friend, no questions asked.

The warrior bond was something to behold and not to be frivolously challenged.

Slipping quietly into his darkened house, Colin closed and locked the door. He walked to the bedroom and as quietly as possible, removed his black flight boots, shrugged out of his shoulder holster, and dropped his flight suit in a pile on the floor.

As he climbed into bed, his wife Janise rolled toward him, her dark hair framing her still youthful and beautiful face. She put her arm around him and whispered in that dusky, sleepy voice that usually affected him like Viagra, "Was it a tough one tonight?"

He just managed a "hmmm" before the need for sleep overcame his desire for sex.

CHAPTER 62

It was late when Dave and Jax returned to the Dungeon. They noted a discreetly placed security contingent protecting the building, probably compliments of the DNI.

Jax told Wiz and Lydia that the hazmat crews were engaged in the containment of the antenna on the roof of the hospital. Barely acknowledging Jax, both were leaning over computers, tapping continuously.

Lydia was building a PowerPoint slide utilizing high-definition, US-controlled satellite photos that Wiz had downloaded for her. She was placing bold red arrows to point out the similarities of the three towers. For contrast, she used bold blue arrows to point out the lack of equipment required to function as legitimate communication links.

"Is there any doubt about whether these towers are fake?" she asked, not for the first time.

"It could be that they just haven't finished them yet," Jax replied, playing devil's advocate.

"Possibly," Wiz said, "but there are no construction vehicles, toolboxes, or spools of cable around the towers. And the portable construction offices have been moved off the job sites. From a contractor's perspective, it looks like the jobs are complete."

"The question is, when are they planning to attack?" asked Jax.

"Lydia, search for the next Muslim holiday," Dave suddenly directed.

After a couple of minutes, Lydia said, "Oh my God. Tomorrow! Tomorrow is Mawlid, the celebration of Muhammad's birthday."

"It's happening tomorrow," Dave said.

They worked late into the night.

Wiz and Lydia collected data and prepared the tower briefing slides for tomorrow while Jax and Dave developed primary and contingency operational plans, including personnel assignments and equipment needed.

After a short night's sleep, all four awakened early without the need for alarms.

Dave gathered them in the Dungeon and described the hastily prepared plan.

When he finished, Wiz and Lydia jumped up and said simultaneously, "I'm going with you!"

"Wiz, I need you to stay here. We will need solid comms and possible real time intel. You have to provide that. We don't have time to staff-up a Tactical Operations Center. You will have to be our TOC. Lydia—we could use you with us. Copy your PowerPoint presentation to a thumb drive. The next few hours could be dangerous. Are you sure you want to do this?" Dave asked her.

"Yes, I'm ready," she answered.

Wiz just nodded. He knew he would be the most effective here, but he still felt an urge to take action, for once wanting the physical confrontation in the field rather than the ethereal battle of the comms center.

CHAPTER 63

From the outside, the Schoolhouse looked like what it was: a sad, abandoned, broken-down building. It was surrounded by a chain-link fence in an attempt to keep vandals and druggies out, and the memories of carefree school days in.

On the inside, it had been restored to a state-of-the-art training facility guarded twenty-four hours a day by armed security.

"The Team" ran the Schoolhouse, among other things.

The Team was a government-funded *consulting* company.

It utilized former Special Forces operators by secretly and strategically placing them in areas of the world that needed a little "help" with resolving internal issues favorable to the United States.

Inside the ramshackle shell of the old school, a twenty-thousand-square-foot pod had been built. It was totally self-contained. There were no windows, so no light escaped. The exterior of the pod's block walls were thickly insulated for sound and painted black. Anyone peeking in the broken windows of the school saw what appeared to be smoke-blackened walls.

Inside the pod, however, everything was brightly lit; the space was clean and had been painted in muted colors. The rooms were designed for different training scenarios, such as hostage rescue and prisoner escape training. There was also a room outfitted with mats for Krav Maga and grappling training. One section even contained darkened rooms for night firing using laser weapons instead of bullets. There were several interview rooms and two large conference rooms.

Dave and Jax were set up in Conference Room Two.

Scotty had arrived early with enough doughnuts for a medium-sized cop convention. He filled the large urn with strong coffee. At 0730, some of The Team began to wander in, all cracking jokes and doing their best to one-up each other.

"Hey, Bobby, tell us again how you shot the windshield of your Humvee while 'cleaning' your pistol." A small roar of laughter erupted from the gathering crowd. They all knew the story, but it was still funny.

"I'm sure it's not nearly as funny as the time your whole team got an emergency call-out at Kandahar Airfield and the twenty-year-old ECP security cop wouldn't let you and the team get to your helicopters on the flightline because you forgot your line badges," Bobby quipped back. Bobby had a point.

Nine special-ops strikers, completely kitted out with weapons, ammo, helmets, and night vision had barreled towards their spinning up Black Hawk and Little Bird helicopters only to be stopped short of the flight line by a young airman demanding to see their line badges.

Of course, none of them had their fucking ID: they were going on a combat rescue mission.

Just as things were getting to the homicidal boiling point, a contractor pilot from a different program had pulled up in his Hilux. He quickly recognized the situation and showed the young airman his line badge that included escort privileges.

"Um, I'm escorting all these guys to the flight line," the contractor bluffed.

The airman, obviously relieved that his life had just been saved, raised the gate and allowed the minivan to careen onto the ramp in a cloud of dust.

The room erupted in laughter at the memory of such times. But as soon as Jax, Dave, and Lydia entered the conference room, the laughter died down and seriousness took over. Lydia sat beside the A/V specialist at the rear of the room and handed him a thumb drive. Jax and Dave marched to the front.

A few whispered murmurs could be heard around the room. "Holy shit, it's him."

Most of the spec ops community knew, or had heard, the legendary tales of Dave Walsh.

Some didn't believe that he was real; some who had worked with him didn't quite believe he was human. But he was respected by all.

Jax didn't waste any time.

At 0800 sharp, he began, "Gentlemen, we have developed credible intel that a significant attack on DC is imminent. We have reason to believe that a foreign interest has placed small, unmanned aerial vehicles carrying Sarin-soaked material on three communication towers. They intend to launch them into the DC area municipal water supply."

"Slide please," Jax said, and the screen behind him illuminated with a photo of the tower on the roof of the hospital. "Last night, hazmat crews removed three, covered, parabolic antennas from a tower recently constructed on the roof of the Children's National Medical Hospital. This tower is designated Tower One. It was discovered that one of the antenna dishes—and possibly all three dishes—contain small UAVs soaked in Sarin liquid. Next slide, please."

A close-up photo of the UAVs nestled in the antenna dish flashed on the screen causing murmurs throughout the crowd of operatives.

"These small UAVs are constructed from a specialized plastic film over foam that is soaked with Sarin," Jax continued. "Once it comes in contact with water, the exterior film melts, exposes the foam, and releases the Sarin.

"You've all had chem-warfare training, so you know the dangers of Sarin. As a reminder, a drop of Sarin the size of a pinhead is enough to kill a human. Sarin off-gasses quickly, but it is persistent on clothing. Also, it easily contaminates water. Dropping these UAVs in the municipal water supply could kill hundreds of thousands. Sarin is also fast-acting: symptoms are evident within a few seconds after exposure. They include violent vomiting, inability to breathe, and severe muscle spasms. I know that sounds like a normal Saturday night for most of you," Jax paused, letting nervous laughter release the tension in the room. "We've identified two other tower sites matching the criteria to possibly contain the UAVs. Slide, please," Jax said as he nodded to Lydia.

The next slide in Lydia's PowerPoint showed two towers identical to the first. Dave took over the briefing. "A tower at this location"—Dave used a laser pointer to indicate a site near the Tidal Basin—"is designated Tower Two. The last tower is in Georgetown, near the Potomac River. It's designated Tower Three. Scott will divide you into two teams to secure Towers Two and Three. We're not clear on how they're to be activated, but we think it will be by remote control since there's no external power source attached to the towers. We feel like the person triggering the attack will have to be relatively close to determine if the UAVs activated. He may be using a handheld device, or even a cell phone like you saw in the desert for triggering IEDs. Today is Mawlid, the Muslim celebration of Muhammad's birthday, and we think this is the day they plan to execute the attack. The precursor to the attack will probably entail the covers of the antennas being blown off."

Dave paused as he let the enormity of the operation sink in. He noticed many of the seasoned professionals showing surprise, a rarity in this crowd of hard-core operators. He continued. "Our mission has two components. First, we sweep the area to find the guy who is going to set the attack in motion and neutralize him. While that sweep is underway, we will climb the towers and secure aircraft cargo straps around the covers to prevent them from being blown clear. That will be a temporary measure until the hazmat crew and cranes arrive to properly contain the antennas. If we are too late and the covers have been blown off, the birds will probably need a couple of minutes to spin up and initialize their navigation units. The UAVs will be vulnerable during that time. One warning: you cannot use water or explosives to neutralize them. Fire is the most efficient method of destroying Sarin; water or explosives will only spread the poison.

"We will attempt to get law enforcement en route to help establish perimeter security, but you may get there ahead of them. Take care that they do not mistake you for the threat. Keep your weapons concealed and make sure you have a liaison to meet the first responders to point out our teams. Questions?"

There were a lot of questions on everyone's minds, but this crowd of professional operatives knew they needed to hold them for the smaller team briefings coming up.

Colin Pierce met Jax, Dave, and Lydia at the front of the room as the other operators moved to the back to meet with their team leaders. They exchanged brief, firm handshakes, and Dave introduced Colin to Lydia. "Where do you need me?" Colin asked.

"How quickly can you get airborne?" Dave asked.

"I've got my sensor operator, Cam, at the airport fueling and conducting the pre-flight. I had him add the two external fuel drop tanks to give us about ten hours loiter-time. We can be on station thirty minutes from when I get to the airport. I should be overhead your operation an hour from now," he said.

"Great. You will be the first one on-site. Start working the perimeters looking for the trigger-men. Check in with the TOC as soon as you are airborne. These are the frequencies we will be using," he said, handing a yellow Post-It-Note to Colin. "The TOC call sign will be Dog Patch," Dave added.

"Copy that. I'm Ghost 91," Colin said.

"Do you have a direct phone line to the TOC? If comms go down, I can call while airborne on my cell," Colin asked.

Dave and Colin swapped phone numbers.

"Thanks, Colin. We'll talk to you in a few. Be safe," Dave said.

As Dave, Jax, and Lydia headed out of the Schoolhouse, Dave stopped and motioned for Scott to join them. "We're going to Tower Two. Give us a call when you get your teams in place," Dave said.

"Roger that. Oh, by the way, I stopped by the Fairfax sheriff's office and was able to convince him to let me retrieve your gear from your truck. Turns out the sheriff and I crossed paths in Afghanistan—small world. He still wants to see you, by the way. I put your stuff in the equipment room," Scott offered as he headed back into the team briefings.

Dave went to the equipment room and began pulling his tactical gear on. Once kitted up, they started toward the truck.

Lydia looked Dave over.

He had on a thick, desert-brown armored vest with weapon magazines fitted into pouches across his chest. Velcroed pockets on the sides of the vest were filled with grenades. A small round light and tiny GPS were clipped to the front of his vest above a holster holding his Glock. A knife was attached to the left side. A long pocket on the back of the vest held a black radio with a short antenna, and a coiled wire ran behind his collar, ending in his ear. Under his left arm, another holster held a smaller pistol.

"You look like Arnold Schwarzenegger," Lydia said. This time, she wasn't grinning.

CHAPTER 64

Ahmed couldn't help but compare their current shabby surroundings to the palace he'd been in only a few days ago. The Budget Hotel in Alexandria, VA, was a long fall from Tarik's Austrian manor and luxurious jet.

The big sign out front advertised "Free TV for only $64 a night."

Tarik had said this location was low profile and was required for operational security.

To Ahmed, it felt like they were already on the run and they hadn't even triggered the attacks yet.

Ahmed's "free" TV in his smelly room showed men in plastic suits swarming around the tower located on the roof of the hospital. They were taking down the covered satellite dishes that contained the little birds with the deadly poison. There was no mention of the other towers.

"They have discovered one of our towers," Tarik stated. "I am sure that pig, Battles, told them about it. It is of no importance. At exactly noon today, we will trigger the other towers. Your cars and drivers are waiting for you in the parking lot. You, Ahmed, will go to this tower," he said, as he handed a map folded to show the park near the Tidal Basin.

248

"Remember your training. You will turn the controller on with this switch. You will then push the flashing green button. You will hear three bangs and see the covers fall away. Once they are clear, the UAVs' engines will begin to turn. It will take four minutes for them to get their navigation fixes. When they are ready, the red button on your box will begin to flash. Once it begins flashing, you are to push the red button and the airplanes will begin flying away from the tower."

He then gave Hamza a map and instructions for his assignments.

Tarik said to them, "Once you have triggered the towers, you are to return to the airport. We will then fly away and watch the chaos reign over this godless land."

"Do you understand?"

"Yes, I understand," Ahmed answered for both of them.

"And you? Where will you be?" asked Ahmed.

"I will be paying Mr. Battles a visit. Do not be late to the airplane. We will leave during all the confusion at 1500 hours. Their security forces will begin closing the airports and we must leave before that occurs," Tarik said.

He handed each of them a cell phone, a knife, and a .22 pistol with a suppressor attached.

"Use the weapons to protect yourself and the mission. At all costs, release the little birds to fly. Once you are successful in your mission, throw your maps, phones, weapons, and controllers in a body of water before returning to the airplane," Tarik instructed.

CHAPTER 65

Cam, Colin's flight engineer and sensor operator had the aircraft positioned in front of the hangar and the pre-flight inspection completed ahead of schedule.

He was leaning against the aircraft, studying his cell phone, when Colin walked up.

"What's up, boss? What are we doing today?" Cam asked.

"It could be messy," Colin replied. "We are tasked with overseeing an operation involving two locations scheduled to go down at the same time." He gave Cam the details from the briefing and a card with the frequencies written on it. "Any problem getting the drop tanks mounted?" Colin asked, as he looked at the ungainly airplane with the two bomb-shaped gas tanks hanging under the wings. Each tank held fifty gallons of Jet A fuel, extending their loiter time by about three hours.

"I was able to get one of the line guys to help me with the bomb loader," Cam said, referring to the hydraulic cradle used to raise the tanks to the wing. The tanks were designed to be jettisoned in flight should the pilot need to lighten his load or decrease drag in case of an emergency.

"Let's go, then. We'll get on station and get the video feed up and running to the TOC," Colin said.

He climbed in the aircraft and secured his harness as Cam began the checklist procedures for engine start.

CHAPTER 66

Battles had to get to his office; he needed to retrieve his "bail-out kit" from the safe.

He'd left in a hurry the day before—as soon as Mona called him—and had used the tire iron from the trunk of his car to break the case of his phone. He then found a drive-thru and ordered an extra-large Coke, made sure his phone was powered up, dropped it in the cup, and watched the lights blink out on it as it shorted out before tossing it in a dumpster behind the restaurant.

He hoped the DNI had not put out a stop and detain order on him with the building security. He was sure the DNI had discussed him with his internal security personnel, but he didn't think the DNI wanted to broadcast that his deputy was crooked. He may have set a trigger for the door entrance that would notify the DNI's internal security when Battles entered the building. They would then quietly take him into custody in the privacy of his office.

Battles waited in the parking lot until he saw a group headed toward the entrance. He got in line with them and "tailgated" through the door without badging in. Normally, that was prohibited, but Battles was the boss, after all, and he looked like he was in a hurry. Going directly to his office without passing anyone in the hall, he entered his office, closed the door behind him, and moved behind his desk as he looked around his office.

Battles had relished the power and control he'd held over the men and women under him for the past twenty years. Now was a fugitive and had to flee.

He'd planned for this day for quite a while but hoped it would never come to this.

Turning to the wall behind his desk, he pulled an oil painting aside and spun the dial on his safe. Inside was a leather briefcase containing two disposable burner phones, a Kimber .45 pistol, one hundred thousand dollars in cash, and his alternate passport and credit cards in the name of Jamison Terry. He also removed a black nylon belt with 32 PAMP Suisse one-ounce gold bars worth about fifty thousand dollars secured in custom-made pockets. He untucked his shirt, fastened the belt around his waist, smoothed his shirt over the belt, and tucked it back into his pants.

Powering up one of the cell phones, Battles began making a series of calls to set up two meetings. His first call was to Tarik.

"Mr. Marshall," Battles said when Tarik answered.

"Yes, and how are you?" Tarik replied, trying to keep the hatred and disdain he felt for Battles from his voice.

"We need to meet immediately."

"I am sorry, but I have a very full schedule today," Tarik replied.

"I don't care how full your schedule is. If you ever plan on leaving this country, you will meet with me in thirty minutes at Corner Bakery. It's about two blocks from the White House.

You will need to stop by a bank on the way because you are going to bring me a down payment on the *investment* we discussed recently. Bring one million dollars in a gym bag."

"Mr. Battles, I am not sure I can get that much cash in that amount of time."

"You will get it and you will bring it to me, or your shiny Gulfstream 550 will never leave Leesburg," Battles warned, referring to the reliever airport thirty-five minutes from Washington, DC, where he knew that Tarik's jet was parked.

"I will try," Tarik spat.

"You will be there," Battles ordered, and disconnected the phone.

Battles then called General Davis and told him to call the other two in their group for an emergency meeting two hours from now at the Army-Navy Club in Arlington.

He looked at his watch. It was 1000 hours. He had a lot to do and little time to do it.

He called Mona.

"The director's office," she answered.

"Mona, I need to borrow your car for a couple of hours."

"Are you in the building? The director is looking for you. I heard him talking to his security personnel yesterday," she whispered into the phone.

"Yes, but just for a minute. The director and I talked last night. It's all just a misunderstanding. We're going to meet this afternoon and clear this up," he said. "So, about your car?"

"Okay. But I'll need it back by this afternoon," she said.

"Meet me in the stairwell with the keys in five minutes."

He took one last look around his office and headed for the stairs. He waited in the stairwell, impatiently, for five minutes before he heard Mona coming down the steps from the floor above.

"Are you in trouble?" Mona asked.

"No, no, I'll meet with the director this afternoon."

"Okay. What do I tell the director if he asks?"

"Tell him you couldn't get in touch with me, but you are still trying."

She hoped he would kiss or at least hug her, but Battles just turned away and started down the stairs.

CHAPTER 67

Jax's phone rang as he was driving. He put it on speaker so that Dave and Lydia could hear.

Caller ID showed it was UNKNOWN, which probably meant it was the Wizard.

Jax answered, "Hello."

"Hey, it's me," said the Wizard. He sounded a little out of breath. "I just got a new feed from Battles's office. He contacted Tarik Basik and called him Mr. Marshall. Battles demanded one million dollars or he wouldn't allow Basik's G550 to leave the Leesburg airport. They're meeting at the Corner Bakery on 14th in thirty minutes.

"Next, Battles made a call to Davis and told him to call 'the other two for an emergency meeting.' He was likely referring to Allen Greensmith and Foster Hillum. He set the meeting for 1200 hours at the Army-Navy Club in Arlington.

"His last call was to someone named Mona, and he asked to borrow her car. She agreed. It's pretty clear he's running."

"Okay. Thanks for that info. Do you have a video feed with Colin and the airplane?"

"Yes, I just got it. He's trying to orbit both towers but they are pretty far away, and it's not very effective. The link is solid, though."

"Do you have good comms with him?"

"Yes. We've already conducted a radio check. We're good."

"Roger that. Have him stay on the two towers," Jax directed.

"Oh, by the way, the pilot has a Cell-Set hooked to his cell phone. He can make and receive calls while airborne. We tested that also, and it's really clear," said Wiz.

"Thanks. Keep monitoring. I'll check back with you soon," Jax said, and disconnected.

"We will never make the Battles and Tarik meeting, but we can make it to Arlington in time for his meeting with the General and SecDef," Dave noted. After a minute, Dave offered, "Let me drop you and Lydia off with Scott. I'll check on the meeting with Battles."

Jax swiveled his head to stare at Dave, "What are you planning?"

"Nothing. I'm just going to talk to them. Maybe arrest them," Dave answered.

He fished around in one of his vest pockets and pulled out a gold FBI badge given to him by an agent as a souvenir for saving the agent's life in Iraq. He affixed it to the front of his vest.

"Ahh, arrest them. Right," Jax said. "Nice badge, by the way."

CHAPTER 68

Dave dropped Jax and Lydia at Scott's truck near the site of Tower Two.

It wasn't lost on Dave that Scott had parked his truck about 100 yards upwind from the huge red and white tower. Dave could see men with climbing rigs preparing to ascend the steelwork to secure the straps on the covers of the three-dish antennas.

Once he was back on the road, Dave called the DNI and advised him that Mona, his administrative assistant, was working with Battles. The DNI responded with some very un-DNI-like language and thanked Dave.

Dave also asked what color and type of car Mona drove. The DNI called back in five minutes; he told Dave that she drove a black 2018 Infiniti Q50S.

Dave drove through the Army-Navy Club parking lot looking for Mona's car, finally finding it in the rear of the lot. Her car was parked near one of the remote, stand-alone meeting rooms built to resemble a small house. He parked and scanned the area: there was no one around. Seeing one of Jax's black windbreakers on the back seat of Jax's truck, he grabbed it and put it on over his tactical gear.

He exited the truck and moved to the corner of the building in front of where Mona's car was parked. The blinds were pulled, but not quite all the way.

Peeking in, he saw Battles, Davis, Greensmith, and Hillum gathered around a small conference table.

A familiar looking muscled guy with an aggressive flat-top style haircut was standing just inside the door. Another sentry guarded the entrance from the outside.

Dave saw a large gym bag in the middle of the table. It was open and several plastic wrapped bundles of one-hundred-dollar bills were visible. Dave had seen lots of money packaged like this over the years. The pile looked to total around one million dollars. On the table beside the bag was a black plastic cube about the size of a sugar cube. It had the same sinister sheen as the piece of plastic they'd cautiously retrieved from underneath the tower.

Dave's plan of action was obvious at that point, at least to him.

Drawing his silenced pistol with his right hand, Dave unclipped the FBI badge with his left and held it in his palm. He slowly moved around to the front of the small building and advanced on the sentry, holding the gold badge out in front of him while hiding the pistol behind his right leg. The badge caused the sentry to pause just long enough for Dave to close within six feet of the sentry.

It took about a second for Dave to smoothly swing the pistol out from behind his leg, aim at the sentry's forehead, and press the trigger.

The suppressed .22 caliber round made almost no noise as it fired. The bullet smacked the sentry's head, sounding like a rock hitting a watermelon. He fell hard against the concrete steps.

Dave moved quickly to the door. He knew Flattop was guarding it from the inside.

He knocked on the door, watching the peephole, and waiting for it to darken as Flattop put his eye to it. When he did, Dave put the silencer over the peephole and fired a round through the glass and into Flattop's eye, shattering his brain. He heard the man collapse to the floor.

Dave took one step back and kicked the door near the knob with a tremendous amount of force, splintering the frame.

The time from when the shot rang out to the door exploding inward was so short, the four men sitting around the table barely had time to push their chairs back and stand up.

Dave stood in the doorway for only a second before Warren Battles said, "It's you!"

Dave quickly looked at each man, raised his pistol, took careful aim, and shot the sprinkler head above the conference table. Before the men could protest, he turned, grabbed the sentry lying on the steps, dragged him into the room, and pulled the door closed.

In seconds, he heard the men begin to cough, followed by loud retching. Their screams continued until the traitors could no longer control their lungs and they fell to the floor, writhing in pain and terror.

Dave walked to the corner of the building and turned the sprinkler system off at the fire department riser. Moving to the side of the building, he unclipped a AN-M14 Thermite grenade from his vest, pulled the pin, released the firing lever, and threw it hard, sending it shattering through one of the glass windows. The grenade made a small splash as it hit the sprinkler-soaked wool carpet, rolled across the room, and lodged against the body of Warren Battles.

The grenade exploded into a 4,000-degree-Fahrenheit supernova, consuming everything in its path, including furniture, bodies, a million dollars in cash, the residue of the Sarin poison cube, and a career-limiting problem for the DNI and the president.

CHAPTER 69

Jax and Lydia stood at Scott's truck and listened to the two-way radio as the team continued to climb the tower. The three climbers were wrapping the aircraft cargo straps around the dish antenna covers to prevent them from opening. Jax heard an aircraft circling overhead and looked up. It was Colin making a wide orbit over the two towers, trying to keep watch over them and provide additional situational awareness for the ground team.

One of the antenna dishes now had three of the heavy white straps around it. The crane was in position and had its long arm extended, ready to attach to the antenna and lower it to a waiting flatbed truck. Just then, the radio in Scott's truck crackled.

"A vehicle is entering the perimeter and is approaching at high speed from the southwest. The vehicle is a dark blue Ford Escape, occupied by two males," Cam, the sensor operator, relayed from Colin's aircraft.

***

Hamza told the driver to park along the side of the road; he'd been reluctant to cooperate with Hamza's requests all day. Hamza felt that the driver had gotten soft from living in this land of fat, lazy people.

They pulled over, and through the open rear window, Hamza saw the men on the tower. It looked like they were putting large straps around the covered dishes that he was supposed to blow off. He took his phone from his pocket and dialed Tarik. "There are men on the tower," Hamza whispered into the phone.

"Blow it now! Do not wait! Blow it now!" Tarik screamed into the phone.

Hamza disconnected the phone and picked up the control box, following the instructions exactly as Tarik had demonstrated. Just as he was about to push the green button, he saw two men walking toward him. One of them had a pistol in his hand; he held it down behind his leg as he walked.

Hamza pushed the green button. The explosive bolts holding the covers on all three dishes fired.

One of the covers that the climbers had not yet secured blew away as designed.

The bolts blew away on the second dish where all three straps were in place, but the cover never moved.

The third dish had only one strap on it.

The climber had just turned back to the ground crew and signaled for them to send up another strap. The timing of his turn saved his life. The bolts on the cover of the third dish blew, sending steel shrapnel into the arms and legs of the climber. Deadly pieces clanged off the steel tower, barely missing his head.

The explosions panicked the driver; he hammered the gas and raced away, throwing Hamza against the seat back. Hamza told the driver to go around the block, but the driver refused to follow his orders. "We need to get out of here!" the driver argued.

"No. We need to get close to the towers again in five minutes. Our mission is not yet complete," Hamza said, in a very low voice, hoping to calm the man.

"No, no. I am leaving. You will have to find someone else to take you," the driver pleaded.

"Okay. Pull over behind that building. You may go, but I will need your car. I will leave it where you can find it later," Hamza said.

"Yes—take the car. You may have it," the driver said, thinking he would report it stolen to clear him of this nightmare. He pulled behind a large grocery store. Both men looked to make sure no one was around. Hamza opened his door, but he waited for the driver to step out of the car ahead of him.

"Here, I have money for you, as promised," Hamza said, as he reached into his shoulder bag. Instead, Hamza pulled out the silenced .22 pistol and fired three times into the man's heart.

A questioning look crossed the man's face as he fell to his knees, holding his hand over the wound producing the excruciating pain. He pitched forward onto the grease-soaked asphalt with his hand still clutching his heart.

Hamza replaced the pistol in his bag and calmly looked around. He saw no one. He rolled the driver over onto his back, lifted him under the arms, and dragged him behind the dumpster. He threw some flattened cardboard boxes over him and then drove away in his car.

Hamza had been gone much longer than the four minutes needed to initialize the little birds. But the controller light was not blinking red. He figured that he must be out of range.

Parking the car about a mile from the tower, Hamza carefully picked his way through the trees until he and the controller were within the sightlines of the antennas. Now that he was back in range, he waited for the light on his controller to flash red so that he could launch the birds.

***

Minutes earlier, as the explosions detonated the covers, Jax and Scott had turned away from the car carrying the two men, their attention diverted towards the tower. When they turned back, the car had raced away.

The crane operator quickly lifted his cable to where the injured man hung from his harness. One of the other climbers moved around the tower, hooked the injured man's climbing harness to the crane hook, and they were lowered to the ground.

Jax knew the UAVs were going to launch at any minute. He needed fire, and a lot of it, to prevent the UVAs from flying and stop the spread of Sarin. He radioed Colin.

"Ghost 91, I need to build a fire—a big one—and fast. Any ideas?"

"Where?"

"At the tower . . . I need to burn the tower to kill the Sarin. The covers have already blown off. We've only got minutes!" Jax relayed.

"Stand by one," Colin replied. "Can you get a flame? A really durable flame going?" Colin asked.

Jax looked around for some type of fire starter. Then he saw it: a set of acetylene bottles being used to cut the steel bolts where the antennas were attached to the tower. "Yes, Ghost 91, I have a flame. But what have you got that will burn?" Jax asked.

"One hundred gallons of prime Jet A fuel," Colin answered. "Get the flame in place!"

The crane operator had just finished lowering the injured man to the ground. The other climbers were down as well and carrying the man to the edge of the field to wait for an ambulance. Jax had the crane operator swing the boom around so he could attach the two acetylene bottles to the hook on the crane. He and Scott quickly hooked the cable to the bottles, opened them both, and used the striker to light the flammable gas. Once lit, Scott forced the brass handle and nozzle into the cable wrappings to keep it activated.

Jax jumped on the crane and yelled for the operator to raise the bottles. He pointed to a spot just in front of the UAVs, their propellers buzzing like angry wasps. The operator positioned the acetylene bottles with the burning torch. Jax then motioned for him to get out of the crane and follow him.

"Are we clear for the drop?" Colin asked Jax.

"Yes. Drop it!" Jax answered, breathing hard as he, Scott, and the operator ran from the crane.

"Cam, on my count, I want you to jettison the two drop tanks at the same time," Colin directed his sensor operator.

"You sure about this, boss?" Cam asked. "I'm pretty certain they weren't designed for this application."

Colin was maneuvering the airplane in a steep dive with the nose pointed directly at the bottles held suspended by the crane. "Yes. I'm sure. It's just like jettisoning them in an emergency, except I'm going to use our speed to give them inertia along a flight path toward the towers."

"Rog, standing by to drop the tanks," Cam said.

Colin was now diving at the max speed allowed for the airplane.

"Ready? On my *mark*," Colin calmly said, over the intercom.

"Ready, ready, ready, *mark*!"

"Away!" Cam reported, as he toggled the TANK EMERGENCY JETTISON switch.

Colin yanked hard on the controls, attempting to pull the airplane out of the dive and clear the top of the tower. It didn't look good. Just as he was certain he was going to collide with the tower, he felt like he had been pushed skyward by a giant hand. With the two heavy tanks full of jet fuel falling free from the wings, the plane's decreased weight shot them skyward. He banked hard to the left, barely clearing the structure, just as the first tank hit the base of the tower.

It cracked open from the impact, but did not explode.

The second tank hit the tower just above the burning torch, the impact vaporizing the jet fuel. It was just what the hungry flame needed. The vaporized fuel exploded into a gigantic fireball, igniting the fuel from the first tank.

***

Hamza's controller began blinking red just as enormous flames consumed the three antenna dishes, melting the UAVs inside them. Seeing that this tower was no longer useful, he returned to the car and opened the second map Tarik had given only to him.

He had one additional mission to complete.

CHAPTER 70

As Dave drove out of the Army-Navy Club parking lot, he called Jax.

"I made contact with Battles's group."

"Did you arrest them?" Jax asked.

"No," Dave answered. "They promised not to do it anymore."

"Where are you now?" Jax asked.

"On the way back. Where are you? Is Lydia with you? Is she okay?"

"Yeah, she's fine. We're at the tower near the Tidal Basin. This site is secure. The crew at tower three at Reservoir Park are onsite and beginning the containment protocol. We're headed to the Incident Command Center at the hospital in about five."

Jax gave the GPS coordinates of tower three to Dave and he entered the numbers into the truck's navigation system. It showed him to be only a few minutes away. Soon, Dave was pulling into the park at the southeast corner of the reservoir.

The tower was easy to spot. It was an eyesore against the verdant settings of the park.

Dave made a cursory scan of the area, noting that the hazmat crew was already on scene. The engine of the huge

269

crane revved as it maneuvered into position. Men had begun climbing the tower. As Dave started towards the man directing the operation, he saw one of the climbers fall; he now dangled precariously from his safety harness.

Dave stopped and scanned the area again. He now noticed a man standing beside a tree at the edge of the field. He had a two-handed grip on a pistol with a long suppressor and was firing at the men on the tower, the noise of the crane masking his shots.

Opting for the low noise signature of his suppressed .22 over the Glock, Dave drew his own pistol and began firing at the shooter. He didn't want to draw attention and have to deal with return fire from local law enforcement.

A .22 caliber pistol wouldn't normally be Dave's first choice of weapon for a fifty-yard duel. Not only did accuracy suffer because of the suppressor, but he was unable to get the shooter to break contact with the tower crew because he couldn't hear Dave's pistol-fire. So Dave unclipped one of his smoke grenades, pulled the safety pin, and tossed it between the shooter and the vulnerable climbing crews.

That worked.

Not only were the climbers temporarily obscured from the shooter, but the terrorist finally realized there was someone else on the field of battle.

***

When the smoke canister erupted, Ahmed turned to his left and saw a big man wearing the equipment of a soldier running toward him with a weapon drawn. Ahmed aimed at the approaching figure and fired off three quick shots.

He knew he would no longer be able to trigger the little birds.

His only chance of survival was to get to the car and escape to the airplane; he began running. Ahmed's driver saw two men with guns racing toward his car. Realizing he was likely going to be in the middle of a shoot-out, he hit the gas and sped off. Ahmed cursed the cowardly driver and shot at the retreating car. Looking for cover, he turned and ran toward a structure near the water, the soldier closing the distance. But every door was locked. Ahmed kicked one open, hoping the soldier would follow him into the building where he could ambush him.

Dave saw the terrorist run to the pump house. He slowed his pursuit when he noticed the broken door and frame. Posting up beside the open door, Dave re-holstered his pistol and removed a flash-bang grenade from his vest. Holding the lever down, he pulled the safety pin and lobbed the grenade, underhanded, into the dark room.

Ahmed heard the grenade hit the floor and knew what to expect.

He'd been in many battles with the Americans and had much experience with their tactics. He immediately closed his eyes tightly, faced the wall, covered both ears with his hands, and opened his mouth to off-set the over-pressure the grenade would produce. The grenade exploded, but Ahmed's tactics had minimized the effects. The terrorist turned immediately after the blast to face the soldier he knew would be coming through the door.

Dave had drawn his pistol and rolled into the room as soon as the grenade flashed. Leading with his weapon, he swept the space for the threat. Dave felt three heavy thuds in the center of his chest; his armored vest had stopped the small bullets meant to kill him.

As he returned fire at the bright muzzle flash of the tango's pistol, Dave could see his bullets ricochet off the concrete walls and the heavy, cast iron water pipes. His weapon clicked empty after four rounds.

The terrorist leaped from behind a large orange shut-off wheel with a knife in his raised right hand. Dave used his left arm to parry the downward thrust and stepped back just long enough to drop his pistol and draw his own knife.

Dave hated knife fights.

Everybody gets cut in a knife fight. It's not at all like the movies. Usually, the one with the least number of cuts wins.

The space was small—not much room for maneuvering—and Dave had his back to the door. He knew the man in front of him would have to kill him to escape.

Dave held the point and cutting edge of his knife along the underside of his forearm. This allowed him to punch, cut, or stab, as tactics dictated.

Ahmed quickly realized that his opponent was no ordinary soldier. *This man has very good training. He has been in combat and hand-to-hand fights before.* He did not sense fear in this enemy; rather, he sensed confidence, patience, and control.

Ahmed lunged at Dave and he smoothly pulled one leg back, easily moving to the side.

Dave countered with an arching slash that cut Ahmed's left shoulder deeply. The knife was so sharp that the cut did not hurt—yet. Ahmed glanced at his shoulder and saw that it was bleeding. He knew blood loss was of great concern and that he must finish this fight quickly before he weakened.

Ahmed made a backhand slash at Dave's right arm, hoping he would move laterally away from the attack to a predicted point so that he could sweep his knife upwards and into the man's stomach. He felt his knife bite through the man's shirtsleeve and skin.

Ahmed loved the feel of his razor-sharp knife slicing through the man's muscle.

For his next move, he would reverse the arc of his knife and stab upwards into the man's gut, under his armored vest.

Dave watched the man's knife very closely. He also watched Ahmed's dark eyes: there was no fear there. *They reminded him of the eyes of the sharks he used to catch when he crewed his uncle's sport-fishing boat.*

Dave's right arm burned from the cut the terrorist had delivered. He knew the man was attempting to get him to step back in order to deliver a fatal stab to the stomach. Instead, he stepped in toward his attacker, taking away the space needed for an upward thrust of his knife.

Dave used his left hand to grab the terrorist's wrist and pin his arm to his side.

The two men were now locked in a death dance.

He could smell the man's putrid breath and see the two-day old stubble on his cheeks. He felt the other man's strength, determination, and sweat as he maintained a vice-like grip on Ahmed's wrist.

Dave's knife was still supported under his forearm as he swept it upward and raked across the man's left jugular vein. Warm blood splashed Dave's face as he reversed the arc and drove the point of his heavy blade through the top of the man's skull.

The downward momentum of the stroke slammed the lifeless man to the floor.

Dave searched the dead man. He had a Jordanian passport with a US visa, along with a map showing the location of the tower, and some type of remote-control device. Dave removed a drop-bag from his cargo pocket and placed all the items, including Ahmed's knife and gun, into it. Before leaving, he used his phone to take a photo of the terrorist's face for later identification.

Dave retrieved his own pistol, inserted a fresh magazine, racked the slide, and holstered it. He jogged back to where the man on the tower had been shot. His teammates had begun combat lifesaving techniques and had the bleeding stopped. Seeing Dave's wound, they used an Israeli bandage from the IFAK attached to Dave's vest to bind the cut tightly, thereby stopping the bleeding. They offered him a handkerchief to clean Ahmed's blood off his face.

After reminding the men how important it was to quickly secure the dishes with straps, Dave raced to the hospital with the injured climber in the back seat of Jax's truck.

CHAPTER 71

Jax, Lydia, and Scott met Dave as he pulled up to the emergency room entrance.

PCAs rushed to Jax's truck and carefully placed the injured worker on a gurney and wheeled him into the ER. Scott followed closely, giving the ER staff details about his man.

Still wearing his tactical vest, Dave put Jax's windbreaker back on before entering the hospital. The FBI badge peeked out from the front of his vest. The deep cut on Dave's arm was painful, but the bleeding had stopped. He knew he would probably need stitches; he would get the doctor to look at it after they'd finished their impromptu debrief.

Scott met Jax and Dave in the waiting area. He had been in the back making sure his two injured men were receiving the proper attention. "The man injured from Tower Two is in critical condition, but he's expected to survive. The man shot at Tower Three is being evaluated and we'll know more about his condition soon. The docs said that whoever patched him up at the site did an excellent job. He may have bled to death without that quick response," Scott relayed to the group.

After a debrief of the day's events, Dave, Jax, and Scott began a lengthy discussion about the reporting process that would be required of them over the next several weeks.

Lydia had no interest in their conversation. She had been riding an adrenaline roller coaster the past few days and was exhausted. Walking away, she sat on a bench just outside the large sliding doors of the ER, tiredly watching ambulance crews wheel the ill and injured into this unique shop-of-horrors.

A place where death and miracles are accepted, equally, as a matter of fact.

She tried to put the last seven days into perspective, but found that she had no basis of comparison—no context that allowed her to understand. It was like she had been living someone else's life. Lydia knew, without a doubt, that the events of the last week had irrevocably altered her. What she didn't know was where she would go from here.

Staring out over the grassy area that separated the hospital grounds from the McMillan Reservoir, she saw a large, tan-colored truck in the distance with FINN HYDRO-SEEDER painted in red letters on the side. A man was on top of the truck spraying a powerful stream of green liquid on the bare ground, effectively painting the brown dirt a bright green.

He was specifically covering the area around a large red and white communication tower that was positioned at the edge of the water.

Lydia would never look at another communication tower the same way after this past week and she noticed now that this tower had the same covered parabolic antennas fairly common to all communication towers.

As she looked more closely at the antennas affixed to the tower, a tumbler in her brain clicked into place. She stood up, walked to the edge of the parking lot, and closely scrutinized the tower that had only three identical covered dish antennas.

Oh, my God, she thought. *This can't be right!*

She turned and ran back into the hospital. Dave, Jax, and Scott were still talking in whispers.

"Give me your phone!" she yelled at Dave, holding her hand out.

All three men were startled.

"Okay," he said calmly. "Are you okay?"

"Give it to me!" She fumbled with it for a minute, then thrust it back to Dave. "Call Wiz!" she almost screamed.

Dave looked at Jax, shrugged, and took the phone back. He scrolled through his contacts, selected "WIZ," tapped CALL, and handed the phone back to Lydia.

"Hey, Dave, how's it going?" the Wiz asked.

"Send me the pics of the other towers!" Lydia demanded, without preamble.

"Lydia? What's up? Why do you need that?" he asked.

"Just send them. Right now!" she yelled, on the verge of hysteria. "Now, damn it. Now!"

"Okay. Okay. Calm down. I'm pushing them . . . now."

The phone she was holding *dinged* with the incoming pictures. She looked at them and disconnected Wiz without a word.

"Oh no. Look!" She held the phone up for them to see the pictures.

"So? What's going on?" Jax asked.

"Come on. Hurry!" she said as she ran out of the hospital.

The men followed her to the edge of the parking lot. Lydia stopped and pointed at the tower by the reservoir, holding up the phone for them to compare the picture of the tower Wiz had sent to the real thing in front of them.

The tower she was pointing at had three antennas, exactly like the ones in the photo. They were all oriented directly at Washington, DC's largest municipal water source, the McMillan Reservoir.

"But that one has cables running to the antennas. The other ones didn't," Jax offered.

"I don't care. They are the same," she said with conviction.

"There were *four* towers, not three! We missed one!" Lydia shouted.

"Call Colin. Get him back on station," Dave directed, as he turned to see Scott already on the phone.

Lowering the phone, Scott said, "He just finished refueling. He'll be overhead in thirty minutes."

"Scott, go get your truck, climbing gear, and a crew and meet us at the tower!" Dave ordered.

"Roger that!" Scott acknowledged. Then he ran toward his truck, parked by the ER.

They all flinched as they heard three successive booms. They looked up just as the covers of the parabolic dishes fluttered toward the ground, and three, near-perfect, ten-foot diameter smoke rings floated upward.

Dave turned to Jax and yelled, "Let's go!"

They all followed Dave as he ran toward the big tan truck. The operator of the truck had just finished loading 1,500 pounds of shredded paper mulch into a 3,000-gallon tank. He had a fuel truck parked alongside, filling the gas tank. A water truck was waiting behind it to fill the mixing tank.

The hydroseeder used internal paddles in the tank to agitate the shredded paper, water, and grass seed, into a thick slurry. The operator would stand on the platform atop the truck, and use the high-pressure nozzle to spray the mixture on the ground.

Dave and Jax kept looking up at the tower as they ran.

They could see the menacing black plastic UAVs attached to each antenna dish. Their propellers were not yet spinning, but the men knew they would start at any minute.

To ensure quick access to his weapons, Dave shed the windbreaker as he ran. He pulled his FBI badge and shoved it in the operator's face.

"I need this truck. Police emergency! I've got to burn that tower!" Dave yelled while pointing to the red and white structure.

Instead of protesting, the operator, named "Red" according to the oval name tag sewn onto his shirt asked, "How can I help? I was an Army Ranger in Afghanistan."

"Have you put water in the tank yet?" Dave asked.

"No. I've got the paper mulch in, but not the water."

"Fill the tank up with diesel fuel instead of water!" Dave ordered.

Red wrinkled his brow, not sure how a hydro-seeder could help burn a tower.

"Hurry! We've only got minutes," Dave said.

Red removed the hose feeding his fuel tank and inserted it into the mixing tank. Cranking the flow rate to the max, he pumped diesel fuel into the hydroseeder. It began to dawn on Red what the FBI guy was trying to do: he was going to use the discharge boom, mounted like a gun on top of the big truck, to spray fuel-soaked, shredded paper. He was going to turn his rig into a giant flame-thrower. Red was sure this had never been tried and he feared that instead of a flame-thrower, they could well end up with a huge bomb.

Red also knew that they would need a source of fire to light the fuel mixture as it left the nozzle. "Flares! Flares! Behind the seat of the truck!" Red yelled down to the guy with the tactical vest and badge.

Dave understood immediately. He stepped up on the running board, opened the door, and folded the seat forward retrieving three road flares and a yellow tie-down strap. He climbed the ladder to the boom platform on top of the truck and used the tie-down strap to secure the flares to the nozzle of the boom.

Jax yelled up to him, "The drone engines have started!"

Dave looked up at the dishes and saw the tiny propellers spinning.

"That's enough fuel. Let's go!" he yelled to Red.

Red shut off the fuel hose and threw it to the ground.

Jax jumped into the cab of the truck and started driving toward the tower. He looked over to see Lydia jump up on the passenger's side running board, holding onto the mirror as he drove across the freshly-painted green dirt.

Dave and Red grasped the railing surrounding the truck's work platform as Jax maneuvered the heavy truck to within 100 feet of the tower. He oriented the rear of the truck and the boom nozzle to face the dishes filled with impending death.

Red yelled to Dave, "I've got to be on the ground to start the pump and agitator. Point the boom like it's a Mark 19," Red instructed, referring to the truck-mounted grenade launcher he had used in Afghanistan. He jumped from the truck and began pushing buttons on the control box. Dave felt the large paddles begin to vibrate the truck as it blended the fuel and paper mixture.

Dave heard a scream. He turned to his left and looked down to see Lydia standing by the rear of the truck. A man was standing behind her with a pistol pressed against her head. Dave swept his Glock out of the holster, immediately obtaining a solid, two-handed grip. He quickly brought the sights to eye level, pointing at the man's head.

Hamza stood directly behind Lydia with his left arm wrapped around her neck as he used her to shield his body. His head was pressed tightly to hers, his finger on the trigger of the pistol.

Hamza motioned with his head for Dave to climb down from the truck. Dave knew the Tango was trying to distract him just long enough to allow the UAVs to launch.

Keeping both eyes open, Dave focused on his front sight. He had the top of the sight superimposed on the tip of the Tango's nose. The pad of his first finger rested against the trigger that he was continuously tightening, like an anaconda squeezing the life out of a rat—not a trigger pull or even a trigger press, just gradual pressure until the spring-loaded striker released and struck the primer of the round in the chamber.

At precisely 3.5 pounds of force on the trigger, the weapon fired, the sights perfectly aligned on the terrorist's nose: no doubt about missing.

Perfect sight picture, perfect sight alignment, and perfect trigger control.

The 9mm jacketed hollow-point bullet exploded out of the barrel, the gun recoiling after the bullet had already left. The bullet traveled faster than the speed of sound with the hostage-taker never hearing the shot. The last thing Hamza saw was the muzzle flash. Eight milliseconds later, the small piece of copper and lead hit him with the force of a four-hundred-pound sledgehammer.

Dave's aiming point, the terrorist's nose, assured the flight path of the round would slice through the brain stem.

The bullet over-pressurized the cranium and blew out the back of his head.

More importantly, the time from muzzle flash to bullet impact was much faster than any human could pull a trigger.

Severing the brain stem ceased all voluntary and involuntary muscle actions, so even with his finger on the trigger, it was impossible for a dead man to pull it. He simply ceased to exist and fell to the ground.

Lydia had screamed again as the man's blood and gore covered her face and hair. Jax jumped from the truck and ran to pull her into the cab of the hydroseeder.

Dave holstered his weapon and stepped back to the truck's spray boom.

Red yelled, "Ready!"

Dave leaned forward and pulled the igniter on one of the flares. It spewed to life and lit the other flares immediately. He pointed the nozzle at the first of the three antenna dishes and opened the discharge lever just as the small UAVs began to detach from their perch.

The high-pressure pump forced the fuel-mulch slurry out of the nozzle at 400 gallons per minute. The flammable slurry passed over the flares and ignited like a huge flame thrower. Dave sprayed a stream of sticky fire in the path of the few UAVs that were just launching. They flew into the maelstrom and melted to the ground. He then directed the jet of fire into the ten-foot antenna openings. The 1000-degree flame melted the UAVs in their nests, destroying the Sarin poison.

In minutes, the high-tech threat had been neutralized by a low-tech solution.

All that remained of the UAVs and the terrorists' dream was the billowing black smoke of defeat.

Tarik could scarcely believe what he was witnessing as he sat in his car in the McMillan Reservoir parking lot. His "secret tower," the one he didn't reveal to Battles, was supposed to be his backup plan if the other three towers were compromised.

Hamza was to trigger the UAVs, but Tarik was standing by with his own controller in case Hamza was captured or killed. Instead, he watched in shock as the soldier on top of the truck fashioned a flame-thrower and rendered all the little birds useless.

His entire plot had failed.

A greasy, sick feeling churned his stomach.

There would be no chaos to cause the stock market to crash. The shorts he'd sold to profit off others' misery would now become the anchors of his ruin. And worse, he would have the full attention of America's terrorist hunters, who were relentless, ruthless, and effective.

Battles—he must have set this in motion.

Hopefully, the little black plastic surprise he'd left in the gym bag with the cash had worked. If not, he would have him killed.

Tarik laid the now useless remote control on the seat beside him, backed out of the parking space, and began the one-hour drive to the Leesburg airport. He called his pilots and told them to prepare the airplane for immediate departure.

CHAPTER 72

Dave climbed off the truck and motioned for Red to follow. They began jogging upwind and away from the tower.

The intense heat of the sticky fire had weakened the steel, causing the tower structure to begin to bend. Just as they joined Jax and Lydia at the edge of the parking lot, the tower fell across the hydroseeder. The tower's jagged, red-hot steel punctured the truck's slurry tank; it erupted into an orange and black fireball.

Red adjusted the cap on his head and exclaimed, "Holy crap! What was that all about?"

Jax patted him on the shoulder and said, "Government business. We'll buy you a new truck."

Lydia still had Dave's phone in her pocket, and it began to vibrate. She pulled it out, her hands trembling, and looked at the caller ID. It was the Wiz.

She handed the phone to Dave.

"Dave," he answered.

"The airplane you had me monitor at Leesburg has some activity. Its registration number is OE-TAH. They filed an international flight plan showing their planned departure is in forty-five minutes," the Wiz relayed to Dave.

"What's the destination?"

"Stand by. Here it is: he filed from Leesburg, Virginia, nonstop, to VIE, which is Vienna, Austria. His flight plan shows eight hours en route."

"I'm on my way."

"Do you want me to call law enforcement?" the Wiz asked.

"No, I'll handle this," Dave said. Then added, "Give me Colin's cell number."

Dave called Colin.

"Hey," Colin answered from the airplane.

"This is Dave. Do you know any of the flight line guys at Leesburg?" Dave asked.

"Of course. They work with us all the time."

"I need you to get them to delay fueling a Gulfstream, registration OE-TAH. Your flight line guys need to claim that their single-point refueler is broken and that they will have to refuel the aircraft over the wing. I need to be there when they refuel that airplane," Dave instructed.

"Roger. I can do that."

"Tell your contact that I'm an undercover FBI agent."

"Copy. I'll call you back."

Dave hung up, retrieved the windbreaker he had discarded earlier, and ran to Jax's truck. He shrugged out of his tactical vest and dropped it on the rear seat as he raced out of the parking lot. His phone rang ten minutes later.

"Go," was all he said as he answered. It was Colin.

"Ask for Leon. He's finishing up college, working part-time at the airport, and trying to get hired with us. We've already vetted him and he's clean. He'll help you out, and he'll keep his mouth shut."

"Leon. Okay, got it," Dave said before he disconnected. Forty-five minutes later, Dave arrived at Leesburg.

Seeing the huge Gulfstream still parked on the ramp, Dave parked Jax's truck near the personnel gate that adjoined the FBO, the private terminal for business aircraft. Putting the black windbreaker back on, Dave leaned back into the truck and rummaged through the center console until he found what he was looking for. He then unclipped one of the small diameter flash-bang grenades from the tactical vest and put it in the right pocket of his jacket. Dave then saw a young man walking over to the entry gate.

"Are you Dave?" he asked. "Colin called and told me you needed to inspect the G550 before we fuel it."

"Yes, I do," Dave answered as he covertly flashed his FBI badge. "Are you Leon?"

"Yes. Colin told me to only fuel the aircraft over-the-wing, and that you needed to be there when I did that."

"That's right. Are you ready now?"

"Yes. I can tell you the pilots are pretty upset over the delay. They wanted the plane to be ready before their boss returned."

With that, Leon tilted his head in the direction of the FBO. Dave could see the two pilots and a third smaller man that he identified as Tarik talking animatedly and pointing from the parked fuel truck back to the airplane. Leon opened the gate and asked Dave to follow him. They walked to the large fuel truck, climbed in the cab, and drove out to the flight line.

"Here, I got this for you," Leon said as he handed Dave a ballcap with the FBO's logo on it. He also handed him a hi-vis vest like the other ramp personnel were wearing. Leon parked in front of and parallel to the big aircraft's right wing.

"I need you to pretend you are training me," Dave said before they got out of the fuel truck.

"Okay, follow me," Leon said, as he stepped down to the tarmac, putting on his best instructor game face.

Dave followed the young man as he made a complete circuit around the airplane, exaggerating his motions as he pointed out how the airplane wheels were chocked and where he attached the grounding strap from the aircraft to the metal ring in the ground. Leon then removed an orange step ladder from the fuel truck and positioned it in front of the aircraft's right wing. He climbed up, placed a rubber mat on the wing, opened the fuel cap, and placed it on the mat.

After climbing down the ladder, Leon returned to the truck to begin rolling out the heavy black fuel hose.

While Leon was occupied with that, Dave quickly climbed the ladder and looked around.

Leon had his back to him; the three men were still engaged in their argument over by the FBO.

Dave reached into his pocket and retrieved the flash-bang grenade.

From his wrist, he removed the heavy rubber band he'd found in the center console of Jax's truck. He double-wrapped it tightly around the grenade's safety lever before pulling the pin on the grenade. The rubber band was the only thing preventing the lever from flying off and igniting it. Dave took one more quick-look around and dropped the grenade into the dark hole of the fuel tank. He heard it splash into the fuel.

Dave climbed off the ladder and helped Leon manhandle the heavy hose as they added almost 4,000 gallons of Jet-A fuel to the tank. Once both wings had been filled, the pilots and owner quickly boarded the airplane. They closed the air-stairs, started the two massive engines, and taxied away.

Dave stood outside the FBO and watched as the fifty-million-dollar luxury jet took off and climbed eastward into the blue afternoon sky toward the Atlantic Ocean.

CHAPTER 73

The glossy white Gulfstream 550 cruised smoothly at .83 Mach through the cold air at 37,000 feet.

The autopilot was engaged, and the pilots were relaxed and watching videos on their iPads. They occasionally looked up at the four large multi-function displays on the instrument panel, checking to be sure that the distance remaining to their destination was decreasing as planned and that they had sufficient fuel to reach their destination. Everything looked nominal.

They were four hours into the flight.

Halfway home.

Halfway across the Atlantic Ocean.

The back of the aircraft was not as relaxed. Tarik was fuming.

He was sure Battles had been responsible for revealing his plans and causing the failure.

If the Sarin cube he'd left in the gym bag hadn't killed Battles, he would begin to make plans to kill the bastard as soon as he landed.

He knew there was still Sarin at the Austrian bunker. He would find a way to retrieve it and make another attack on the American infidels. It was his destiny.

At exactly four hours, twelve minutes, and eight seconds into the flight, the rubber band that had been slowly dissolving in the jet fuel while holding the safety lever of the flash-bang grenade in place finally broke, allowing the lever to actuate. The strong spring on the striker forced the striker to rotate upward, moving the lever out of the way as it drove the fixed striker pin into the primer charge, exploding the grenade.

The flame produced by the grenade submerged in the remaining 1000 gallons of fuel created a tremendous explosion that blew the right wing completely off the airplane.

The pilots never had a chance to react, though they could have done nothing. They were immediately jerked sideways as the 60,000-pound jet rolled hard-over to the right. The sudden lateral change of direction at over 550 knots snapped both of their necks.

In the rear of the aircraft, Tarik was thrown violently from his huge captain's chair. His left arm broke as he instinctively reached out to cushion his impact. The centrifugal force of the spinning aircraft kept him pinned against the ceiling of the airplane.

He was unable to do anything except scream for the four and half minutes it took before the left engine, still running at full power, slammed the wildly spiraling jet into the surface of the ocean, shredding every part and person aboard into tiny pieces.

The debris field floated for a while, then ingloriously sank into the icy depths of the Charlie-Gibbs Fracture Zone, finally coming to rest on the seafloor 14,700 feet below the surface.

CHAPTER 74

Three days later, Dave, Jax, Lydia, and the Wizard were sitting in a small waiting room just outside the president's Oval Office.

Dave and Jax looked very professional in dark suits, starched white shirts, and striped ties. Lydia was wearing her "intern disguise"—the name she'd bestowed on the outfit for the fake interview with Battles. The Wizard was another story: he didn't own a single pair of hard-soled shoes and had only worn a tie when making fake ID photos.

So, Jax and Lydia had taken him shopping.

It was like giving a cat a bath.

After spending most of the day at the mall, they had settled on a dark blue blazer, khaki pants, penny loafers (in which he had placed two shiny pennies, heads up, as soon as he got them home), a blue oxford shirt (purchased one size too big so the buttoned collar didn't "strangle" him) and a clip-on tie.

The Wiz pulled at the collar of his shirt with his finger the entire time they sat waiting.

None of them spoke; even Dave and Jax seemed a little subdued.

The door to the room opened and a young man with perfect hair and teeth and wearing an expensive suit entered. He carried a black leather binder under his arm and introduced himself as Sean.

"We are ready to go in. Please only speak when spoken to. Do not ask any questions. The president or the DNI will do most of the talking. Only offer to shake hands if the president offers his first. Address him as Mr. President. I will show you where to sit. Do not lean back on the couch or cross your legs or arms. Stand up when the president enters the room. Any questions? No? Good. Let's go," he motioned for them to stand by raising both his hands, palms up.

Sean looked intently at Wiz for a moment, then rummaged in his jacket pocket and fished out a napkin. He extended it to Wiz's face and waited while the Wiz spit his gum into the napkin. Folding the used napkin with poise, Sean returned it to his jacket pocket.

The aide turned his back to the group, shot his cuffs out of the end of his suit jacket sleeves, and began marching toward the door. Dave and Jax looked at each other and grinned, both thinking, *where do they find these guys?* as they followed him into the Oval Office.

Lydia looked around the immaculately decorated Oval Office. With its rounded walls, wooden desk set against the floor to ceiling windows, and the Presidential Seal woven into the carpet, the room looked like a movie set. A week ago, Lydia had been running for her life with someone else's blood on her; today, she was going to meet the President of the United States.

Sean pointed them to two identical couches that faced each other. He motioned Dave and Jax to one couch and Lydia and the Wiz to the other. Within minutes, one of the curved doors opened and the president entered the room with the DNI trailing behind.

The president had a big smile, showing lots of white teeth.

All four visitors shot to their feet.

The president had his hand extended before he even reached his guests. He shook Jax's hand first.

"Jackson, how are things at 'The Group?'" he asked.

"Fine, Mr. President."

"Good, good. And Dave, how are you?" the president asked, extending his hand again. "It's been a while since we last met. I guess retirement is a little more active than you anticipated," he said, drawing a sideways glance from Jax. Dave had failed to "mention" that he had met the president before.

"I'm fine, sir, and yes, it's not quite the sedate life I had heard about."

The president laughed genuinely while shaking Dave's hand and pounding his shoulder, causing Dave to wince from his recent knife wound.

"Oh, I'm sorry . . . I forgot you were wounded. Does it still hurt?" he asked.

"No, sir; I'm good," Dave replied. *You should have seen the other guy,* he almost added.

The president said, "You must be Mr. Grant," as he firmly shook the Wizard's hand.

"Yes, sir. How are you, sir?" the Wiz said, immediately breaking protocol by asking a question. Sean, standing quietly in the corner, rolled his eyes.

The president laughed, and answered, "I'm fine, thanks to the four of you."

He moved to Lydia and offered his hand. "Miss Berkley, I hear you've had quite a week."

"Yes sir," was all she could offer.

"I want to apologize to you two," he said, looking at Lydia and the Wiz, "for dragging you into a 'family squabble,' as it were."

"Sean, can you give us the room?" the president asked the aide, which was a polite way of saying "You need to leave now because we are going to talk about things you are not cleared to hear."

"Yes sir," Sean answered. He exited the room, quietly clicking the door shut behind him.

The DNI took a seat on the couch beside Dave and Jax, while the president pulled a chair up to the end of the couches so he could address everyone at once. He made eye contact with everyone before he began.

"The director gave me a full briefing of the events that occurred over the last seven days—at least, as full as I need to know. You four have my and the country's sincerest thanks and appreciation.

"The unfortunate fire at the Army-Navy club prevented us from bringing the perpetrators of some very serious crimes to trial. Your intervention in stopping the Sarin attacks will never be publicly known.

"It appears that shoddy construction caused a couple of those towers to be destroyed by an electrical fire." He looked around the room to make sure everyone was on board with the spin he was putting on this near disaster. He saw all four heads nod in agreement.

He stood up, walked to his desk, and returned with four small black cases, presenting one to each of his guests. "On behalf of a grateful nation, I wish to offer this token of appreciation for your heroic actions."

They opened the silk-covered boxes to reveal the Presidential Medal of Freedom. The white enamel five-point star was mounted on a gold badge and had a dark blue ribbon with a small white strip on the edges.

"That is the highest award this country can bestow upon a civilian. Unfortunately, because of the secrecy of this operation, we will need to hold them in 'safekeeping' for you," he said. The DNI then collected all four medals to be placed in a vault in his office.

"However, there are some tangible things we can do for you that will be revealed at a later date. For now, know that I am forever indebted to each of you for your bravery and the actions you took to protect this country. If you ever need anything from this office, please call for me. My personal secretary will have your names, and she will give you a private line to call.

God bless each of you."

With that, the president stood up.

Everyone else stood up too.

After one more round of handshakes, the DNI led them out of the Oval Office.

CHAPTER 75

The DNI had a limousine waiting to take them to his office.

As they entered the director's offices, Dave and Jax noticed that Mona's desk had been cleaned out.

A small tray of pastries sat on the director's conference table. Coffee, water, and tea were on a side table. The Wiz was on his second doughnut by the time everyone else took their seats around the conference table. He had already removed his clip-on tie and stuffed it in his jacket pocket.

The DNI began, "I can be a little more candid than the president was able to be. This situation could have been a disaster for the country and the administration. The fire at the Army-Navy Club solved a lot of problems," he said, making and holding eye contact with Dave. "No one has heard from Tarik Basik since he left the Leesburg Airport; there are no reports of his Gulfstream landing. Air Traffic Control reported they lost contact with his aircraft about four hours into his flight over the Atlantic Ocean. They think he turned the transponder off so that he could not be tracked. Our intelligence community will continue to monitor aircraft databases. It's pretty difficult to hide a Gulfstream G550. If he's in circulation, we will find him."

No one spoke, and he continued. "One of our intelligence operatives informed us of the discovery of a former Nazi underground chemical plant near Linz, Austria. That plant was the source of the Sarin. It was formulated over eighty years ago and then preserved and packaged so well that it was still viable. We have a team embedded with the bunker exploration crew on the ground in Austria at this time. We will control whatever Sarin is remaining.

"We have also been unable to locate Tarik's sister, Amina. She was the nanny for the professor who was involved with the initial discovery of the Sarin. The professor and his entire family, including the two young children under Amina's care, were killed in order to gain access to the Sarin. We think the killers were the two men who attempted to trigger the towers here."

The DNI turned to Lydia and said, "Lydia, I'm sorry you got pulled into this. These three guys"—the DNI nodded toward Dave, Jax, and Wiz—"say you are very good with computers and that you have good operational instincts. I trust their judgment and would like to offer you a job working with us at the DNI. We will secure housing for you, enroll you in a local university, and pay you a salary. You will work at the Dungeon with the Wizard on the days you are not in school."

Lydia smiled and the men laughed at the director's use of the Wiz's nickname, as well as "Dungeon" for the Wizard's operational headquarters.

"Thank you, sir. Yes, I would like that," she said quietly, afraid this was all a dream.

"Good. We need you and your skills."

"As for Mona, she has been reassigned to a transportation repair center as a service writer. It will take a while to sort out all the damage Battles caused, but we are slowly peeling back the layers on that. In the interim, we have asked the former DDNI to come back and help us. Dave, your old boss, Alexandria O'Shannessy, was perfect in this job—lots of operational experience and a reputation for being tough, but fair. She has agreed to come out of retirement and help me pick up the pieces.

"In addition, the president has directed that we assist you in rebuilding your house, Dave. He feels it was torched due to the actions of rogue government officials. He also asked if you would agree to return to part-time service as an independent contractor, working with Jax on special projects. You can name your salary and your working schedule."

"I'll need to think about that," Dave answered.

"Fair enough. We can wait for that answer."

The DNI turned to the Wiz. "Young man, you've had the sword of Damocles hanging over your head long enough. You've more than earned your freedom from us, if you want it. I know you could probably make a lot more money building video games on the open market."

For once, the Wizard thought about his answer before speaking. "No, sir. I think I like what I'm doing. However, it is nice to know I will be doing it by choice."

The Wizard wondered why no one had mentioned the roughly 120 million dollars he had hidden for them in ether-space.

CHAPTER 76

Dave stood still, watching the sky darken as the western horizon began to take on a pink glow. He could hear the crickets rattle their legs and a trio of baritone bullfrogs performing at the nearby pond.

It was a late Saturday afternoon and he was alone at his house, or what was becoming his house. He smelled the fresh pine scent of the new lumber and looked through the vertical wood studs at the late summer fields of fescue, ready to be cut and baled. Dave had decided to rebuild on the same spot where his former home had burned. Weeks earlier, work crews had bulldozed the charred timbers, along with some of his memories, into a pile that they hauled away and buried in a landfill.

Dave saw headlights bouncing down the drive toward his house and couldn't help himself; he instinctually calculated the time it would take him to get to his truck and retrieve a weapon. Mental math told him that with the light levels as they were and the speed the vehicle was traveling, he would be able to recognize the make and model with enough time to make the short trip to his truck.

Within two seconds, Dave was able to determine it was the Wizard's new red Ford Raptor. In another three seconds, he could see there were two occupants in it.

Another two seconds after that, he could tell that the Wiz had Lydia with him.

Gravel sprayed as the Wiz slid to a stop in front of the house. The 8" lift kit and monster tires held the body of the truck so high off the ground that they both had to jump down.

Lydia looked fresh and happy, like a young college girl.

She ran up to Dave, slung her arms around his neck and hugged him tightly, like a daughter hugging her dad. *Like Sarah.* Dave closed his eyes and hugged her back.

She and the Wiz had become an item of sorts. He fed off her street smarts, and she fed off his geek smarts. They were both enjoying each other's company.

Lydia turned and walked through each barely defined room. Even with the walls only framed with wood studs, she seemed to be able to read each space. She slowly viewed the area, seeing in her mind the walls, the paint colors, the windows and curtains, the carpet and furniture.

She smiled her approval after her virtual tour.

Finally, she turned to Dave, flung her arms wide, and said, "I love it!"

And for the first time in a long time, Dave did too.

ABOUT THE AUTHOR

Steven Canter spent nearly two decades as a Program Manager and pilot for Lockheed Martin's renowned Skunk Works. During that time, he managed to survive numerous deployments to austere locations. Unwitting is his first novel.

Made in the USA
Coppell, TX
26 May 2021